Praise for *Annihilation for Beginners*

"Charlie Stephens's people are precisely the people we need right now—complex, compassionate, queer, courageous, and just a little bit sick of the way people focus on what is entirely beside the point. They have what the wise old woman who raised me would call gumption. I would follow this writer into any dark woods." —**Pam Houston**, author of *Deep Creek: Finding Hope In The High Country*

"Charlie J. Stephens's stories move deftly through Oregon's varied landscapes—coastal fog, high desert, ancient groves—where the natural world offers something like kinship to those navigating loss and its long tail. These are characters raising reptiles, getting strange in cemeteries, asking themselves why they're still here and finding the answer in unexpected anchors: a child, a snake, a stranger's kindness. Stephens writes with wry philosophical weight and a dark wit, turning the dread we all carry into something oddly beautiful and life-affirming." —**Kimberly King Parsons**, author of *We Were the Universe*

"Sometimes you find a book that stays with you—one that delights as much as it haunts. I loved every single page of *Annihilation for Beginners*." —**Betsy Gaines Quammen,** author of *American Zion: Cliven Bundy, God & Public Lands in the West*

"These solid, beautiful stories break open like exquisite geodes. Populated by a spectrum of characters who find themselves in less-than-ideal situations and locations, *Annihilation for Beginners* shows us that beneath our rough exteriors, eroded by loss and longing, often lie hidden, tender interiors shaped by a desire to know ourselves and how we fit into the vast, unknowable world that surrounds us." —**Evan P. Schneider**, author of *Rural Education*

"Stephens's sensitivity to nature and the human condition is exactly what this world needs. These stories mesmerize and hold you, even when everything feels impossibly damp and socked in. You'll laugh, cry, and emerge remembering that it isn't so bad to be a human being—so full of hope and so full of wonder." —**Erin Steele**, author of *Sunrise Over Half-Built Houses: Love, Longing and Addiction in Suburbia*

"Charlie J. Stephens is a bard of the Oregon coast, the Willamette River, the people left behind and the people doing the leaving, the transplants to the city's edges, the birds and deer and trees, the broken link between human and humane. This is a book about queer solitude and dreaming, the potential of friendship, the persistence of childhood longing, and what it means to grow. Each story stands on its own, while together they build up to a crescendo of conflicting feelings, 'the momentum underneath everything.'" —**Mattilda Bernstein Sycamore**, author of *Terry Dactyl*

Buckman Publishing LLC
est. 2018
1448 NE 28th Ave
Portland, Oregon 97232
buckmanjournal.com

Congratulations! A Buckman production is in your hands! We're an unorthodox operation that continues the daredevil tradition of literature, printing new sparks that ignite imagination. Proudly independent, Buckman's defiant attitude aims to inspire and increase readership in greater society.

READ THIS BOOK WHEREVER BOOKS CAN BE READ

Words © 2026 Charlie J. Stephens
Cover & Artwork © 2026
Julianna Bright
Book Design: Ellen Robinette
Typefaces: Garamond Premier Pro,
SARABUN, **Wayfinder CF**

ISBN:
9781967058068
LCCN:
2026930175

No part of this publication may be reproduced or transmitted in any form—electronic, mechanical, photocopying, recording, or otherwise—without prior written permission of the publisher.

This is a work of fiction. Names, characters, places, and incidents either are the products of the author's imagination or are used fictitiously. Any resemblance to actual persons, living or dead, businesses, companies, events, or locales is entirely coincidental.

Buckman operates from our home in the upper left of Turtle Island at the confluence of the Whilamut and Wimahl rivers, among the waters and lands of the Cayuse, Clackamas, Multnomah, St'pulmsh (Cowlitz) Umatilla, Walla Walla, and Watlala peoples.

ANNIHILATION FOR BEGINNERS

STORIES BY CHARLIE J. STEPHENS

For everyone staying tender through the apocalypse. For everyone fighting like hell.

Forgive yourself for not knowing what you didn't know before you learned it.

—**Maya Angelou**

I knew that the real was yonder and that the darkened dream of it was here.

—**Black Elk**

TABLE OF CONTENTS

COAST
Black Arion—14
A Day at the Beach—19
Those Coyote Teeth—29
I Am a Conservationist—39
The Wind—43
Gymnogyps—71

RIVER
Willamette—82
A Home in Beaver Palace—92
Tyranny of the Quantifiable—101
What the Ex Broke—103

FOREST
Look Up—108
King—118
I Am Right Here—122
Just This—127
For the Birds—130

VALLEY
The Sheet—142
The Owl People—144
Each Motion a Promise—154
Annihilation for Beginners—157
The Parent—161

SKY
The Red-Eye—168
Zeus's Fear—171
School of Velocity—173
It's a Big World—176
The Vulture—179
Something Divine—181
Push Me Away a Little Closer—188

Black Arion

Daisy is a show pony and she always has been. She's got the pompoms, the leotard, the hip-hop dance class at the YWCA, the youth theater auditions, the singing lessons, and the piano recitals. She's got the special smile she uses when there's a camera nearby and she says *Please* and *Thank you* without ever having to be reminded. She's only nine now, two years younger than me, but I don't feel like I've got any kind of firstborn clout here.

My family lives near the ocean, and the salt air eats away at the foundation of our house each winter, but this is not something Daisy would ever notice. While she's pliéing in the kitchen, I'm studying the way everything under us is cracking apart, splintering, and coming undone. There are fractures on the patio, and the walls sometimes seem to swell and sway, barely able to stand the pressure.

Sometimes when Ronny, my stepdad, is out with his friends, and Mom is at work, and Daisy is looking at herself in the mirror or whatever she does, I go down into the basement. It's cold down there, so it's best in the summer. The slugs all move in for the moisture, crawling along the damp floor, leaving trails of silver. The main kind of slugs we have are the shiny ones called Black Arions. I looked them up, found out they're hermaphrodites. I wasn't sure what a hermaphrodite was, not really, so had to look that up too. Sometimes when I look up stuff, I tell Ronny and he's usually impressed that I know so much, but this isn't something I want to explain to Ronny.

Earlier this summer there was a day when everyone was out, and I did something I'd been thinking about doing for a long time. I went to the basement, took off all my clothes, and laid down in the middle of all the slugs. It felt like hours, waiting. A lot of them came close then stopped, curled up, or changed directions. But then finally one and then another slowly made their way up my side, crossing the landmass of me. I tried to stay completely still, pretended I was a corpse. I wondered what we looked like as their cold bodies glided over mine, wondered what someone would think if they walked through the door and saw. Then I imagined it was me coming through the door, looking down at my own body. Flat chest, slender hands and feet, and all my pet slugs around me, a whole kingdom. I saw myself and thought, *Here's someone who is interesting at least.*

But I'm not sure anyone else would agree.

Now, I can't get the idea of a hermaphrodite out of my head. I feel distracted by it all the time. Wonder if I know any hermaphrodites. Sometimes I think Ronny might be a hermaphrodite. Once I saw him in Mom's dress and they were laughing in the bedroom and closed the door and kept on laughing, and they never said anything about it later. Mom could be one too. She's got these thick hairs above her lip that she sometimes forgets to pluck and when they grow out there's a dark shadow there.

My dad left us when I was one, and I don't remember him. Mom says I don't need to worry about him because I got her genes. She said before I was born, she thought I might come out black, because he was black, but I'm almost as white as her, prone to sunburns. I did have dark, curly hair like him when I was little but it has lightened—Mom says with the sun—and softened over time. I wish I had something from him, something I could point at and say, "See, this is from my dad."

Daisy is my half-sister, but I've known her almost my whole life. Sometimes I feel bad just calling Ronny my stepdad because he's been here for so long. Daisy has all the luck. She's good at everything, has two parents who made her on purpose, and she's pretty in a way that people recognize, even just on the street. When she was younger, and some stranger would say how cute Daisy was, Mom would always correct them.

"She's not cute, she's INTELLIGENT," Mom would tell them, and give them the eye.

Most people didn't seem to understand, probably were horrified that this mother was yelling in the grocery store about how her daughter wasn't cute. People generally haven't exclaimed about my cuteness, but I do get some attention. Mom says I'm precocious, and when she says it I know I have something Daisy doesn't have. This past year, right before school let out, I got sent to the office because the teacher told us to make Father's Day cards, and I told her that her assumptions about the nuclear family were misguided. She just stared back at me with her round mouth open like a cave, and I could see her gold fillings in the back, before her lips got hard and tight and she told me to leave the room. The principal called home, but that night when she got off work, Mom just gave me a big hug.

"The nuclear family is misguided, huh?" she asked me before lights-out, as she leaned in my doorway, rolling herself a cigarette.

I told her that a few months back I had heard her talking with her friend Francis—that I'd sat in the hallway and listened as they drank wine and blew smoke out the window.

"Francis said nuclear families were nothing to strive for and were often pretty dysfunctional," I reminded her. Mom smiled and gave me this look she gives me sometimes.

"I'm scared to ask what other conversations you've eavesdropped on," she said, laughed a little, and turned out my light.

But I couldn't sleep. I wondered what else Mom talked about with Francis when they thought no one was listening. Sometimes when I can't sleep, I think about the Black Arions in the basement, living their hermaphrodite lives. I picture their slick black bodies, their movements so slow and sure. If I visualize them long enough, I can usually fall asleep. Sometimes though, I just keep worrying about things. My biggest fear is that I'll just grow up to be a regular woman with boobs and kids and stresses. I don't want that, not at all. My friend Imani just got a bra and I can tell she is so proud of it, like she's getting somewhere, like she's grown up. I don't mind that she's excited, but I don't have much to say because that's the last thing I want. I don't want to explain anything though because I might end up telling her about the slugs and she wouldn't understand. I can't think of anyone who would understand. Not Mom, not Ronny, and definitely not Daisy. I wonder if my dad would understand somehow, like maybe he left because he agreed that a nuclear family wasn't all that great, and maybe he was precocious like me and wouldn't think it was weird if he knew about me and the Black Arions.

I thought everyone was out again today when I went to the basement. I took off my clothes and laid down in the spot I liked, near the window that looked out at the yard at eye level, so I could see the overgrown grass and the ocean winds blowing the cedar tree. There was just one Black Arion out, and it was curled in a ball of silver it had made. I curled in a ball too. Then it stretched out a little and moved, and I tried to copy what it did exactly. I wasn't thinking of it as a dance, but for a second I could understand why Daisy liked to practice her assemblés and arabesques over and over. I stayed on the floor for a while, making the same shapes as the slug, but I was getting cold. When I pushed myself over, I saw her feet first, housed in pink ballet shoes, and when I looked up, there was Daisy, staring at me with a look on her face that made my stomach turn icy.

"Mom! Dad!" she screamed, strangely guttural and hoarse, in a terrified voice I'd never heard her use before. "Help!" like it was an emergency.

Mom and Ronny came running down the stairs, stopping next to Daisy a few feet away from me. I just stayed still before them, shivering and naked.

No one said anything at all.

Below us, the Black Arion stretched itself out, slowly covering everything in silver, looking like it was having the time of its life.

A Day at the Beach

I thought Jude was flirting with me at the cafe, but then she started telling me how some Tibetans believe that we've all lived so many previous lives that everyone we pass on the street was once a mother or a father to us. Beautiful, yes. But not too sexy.

It was okay, I still had some hope regarding Jude. Even though someone in middle school (over thirty years ago now—apparently these things have a way of sticking with you) told me that my face looked like the bottom of a bucket, I was not without my charms. I tried to remember that, especially in situations like this. My older brother Victor tried to protect me from the biggest bullies, including our parents, but even he couldn't prevent the mean world from seeping in.

"Clem," he used to tell me, "you're not like other girls, but that's your superpower. Don't let them make you think they're better than you because they're not." He was always good at seeing something in me that I couldn't. He was like that with everyone.

It was my day off, so I walked along the muddy river to the ocean with my mid-morning coffee, still thinking about Jude even though Jude probably wasn't thinking of me. I thought of Victor too. If he was still alive, he'd be the person I'd most want to be on the beach with today, how much he would appreciate it. The dark evergreen trees were magnificently bored—no wind—and the water was a glass mirror, reflecting everything. The dark, gray sky sat heavy and low, and I was breathing in whole clouds. They floated around and pressed up underneath my rib cage, trying to get back out.

Near a stand of pampas grass, two parents in winter coats and ski hats set up optimistic beach chairs in the damp air and watched their two half-naked kids run around in the sand, impervious to the cold. The children jumped in the roaring Pacific and climbed on driftwood, whipped the sky and their legs with bull kelp and threw rocks and sand at the waves and at each other.

I found a sturdy piece of driftwood to sit on, felt the smooth wood underneath me. I watched the waves, watched the horizon, and watched the kids doing all their unpredictable kid things. The little boy was probably six, and the girl was maybe nine. I'd never wanted kids of my own, but they're fun to watch from a distance, kind of like going to the zoo. The younger one started crying and rubbing his eyes—pointing at his sister with a snarl—it was probably a handful of sand that got him.

Jude is our small town's only therapist, and even though I would benefit from some help working through the old traumas I still carry around, I was holding out because of the ethical clause that therapists can't be romantically involved with their clients. There's another therapist one town over, about an hour's drive away, but he's a pinched old thing—very Freudian—so I decided to just keep trying to work out my problems on my own.

Jude's got the lean, sturdy body of a forest rabbit and has crooked little teeth I regularly find myself wanting to run my tongue across. She often seems a little unkempt with her wild hair she lets fly every which way, and the loose clothing, like she's in disguise, hiding a secret. She lives alone above town on the bluffs, in a little blue house that's mostly windows. I've been to parties she's thrown there over the years, where we've talked and laughed so easily, on varied topics most people don't have the patience for. Once, a few years ago, we even watched the sun come up together, listening to Joni Mitchell on her old record player and having so many feelings. Or at least I think we were. She comes so close, and I can feel her pull and reach and want, but she always decides to disappear in the end. It's been like this for a long time. I'm not sure why I haven't given up on Jude. There's just something about her.

I'd been looking out at the waves, watching them crash mightily against the cliffs, and was still thinking about Jude so my guard was down. The mother from the beach-chair family was already too close when she startled me by clearing her throat. She was dragging along her older child, the girl, who had red hair, a reddened face, and red short-shorts—everything flecked with dark sand now—her eyebrows scrunched together in a tight knot. Actually, they both had tight knots between their eyebrows—two grimacing twins here to tell me something. The mother spoke first.

"My daughter Bianca is very sensitive and she acts out when she can feel someone's energy too strongly." She stared at me waiting for a reply, like this was the most normal conversation-starter in the world. Their four eyes were a steely green-gray, trying to pierce right through me.

"I'm just enjoying the ocean," I said. "It's my day off."

"Well, her force field extends about fifty yards in every direction."

"Force field?"

Bianca stood there, still as a statue, but her mood had shifted.

A feral smile tugged at her upper lip. I couldn't think of anything more mortifying than to be her right now, but she seemed to be enjoying herself.

"You're wanting me to move farther away," I said, already knowing the answer so it wasn't really a question.

"Just down to the next rocky outcropping. It's not that far."

She pointed with a limp wrist like she was royalty, having come to our little Oregon beach town to regale us—her long, painted fingernail sharp at the tip. Bianca and I looked down the beach to see what she had in mind. "Otherwise our day will be ruined," she said. "Bianca can't help it—she just feels so much. She gets it from me."

I wanted to be outraged, but unfortunately I understood exactly what she meant. I knew this overwhelm of feeling but it had never occurred to me to demand space for myself. I nodded at them, pulled my jacket tighter around my chest and stood up.

"You should work on that," the mother said as an afterthought, when I was already a couple steps away. "Your energy is very strong. Stronger—and to be frank—*stranger* than most. Bianca and I usually can't feel someone from so far away. It's...it's just too much. I'm not sure how you manage."

I had the fleeting thought they might be a family of aliens, here on Earth to experience base human emotions, to investigate everyone they meet, running their tests and making mental notes. I took one more look at Bianca who was openly grinning now—she had unsettlingly straight, white teeth that looked to have been made in a factory. I decided not to respond to the mother. Bianca seemed to be fine standing near me even with all my supposed energy, but I didn't want to waste my time pointing that out. Without another word I turned away from them to walk towards the new vantage point the mother had chosen for me. I could feel their eyes on my back like sharp little pinpricks.

The thing is, it wasn't the first time I had heard some version of this. One of my last lovers—not as hard to come by in a small town as one might think—told me I had pulled her like a magnet, like it was purely energetic and she didn't have a choice. She made it sound so non-consensual, which wasn't ideal.

"You're at your most attractive very close up," she said more than once, her lips vibrating against mine as she spoke, eyes wide open, seeing my every pore. "From farther away you can't see and feel this special thing you have."

We broke up after only a few months. While such a situation would have been ideal in my twenties, it felt unsustainable to be with someone who only found me appealing at a half-inch or less apart. The sex we had was hard to say goodbye to, I'll admit, but it wasn't enough to keep going.

The sand gave way under my shoes as I walked down the beach, and the waves came up to greet me, coming so close and sneaking away, just like Jude. I didn't mind. I walked past the towering rock arch with its thick encrustation of barnacles exposed at low tide. I leaned over to listen to them chirping and squeaking. I told them, as I always do, that they're my favorite musicians. The barnacles' song almost always lifts my mood—more than the birds and the frogs—who can sometimes sound so forlorn. The barnacles' high-pitched chorus sends the nerves at the base of my skull tingling, and my whole body feels lighter. I've had the thought that when I retired, I'd have time to sit next to them each day at low tide—if they're open to outsiders like me—and take the time to understand their language, to finally comprehend the gorgeous little messages they're sending.

When I got to the rocks the mother had pointed me towards, I thought about sitting elsewhere just to spite her, but really, it was a perfect rock to sit on. I was surprised I'd never noticed it before—black with streaks of gray veins, and a curve that fit my butt as if it had been made for me. For some reason I started thinking of that mean middle school boy who had said that thing about my face. It was such an odd thing to say, but rather creative really, in hindsight. I couldn't remember his name. Conrad or Cody. I do remember he had a mullet and was the first boy in our grade to have his little mustache hairs sprout. It occurred to me that maybe someone had told him his face was bucket-like, and he was trying to pass it along. I imagined him now, middle-aged—mustached, bearded and still mulletted—and wondered if he was happy, if he liked his life and what he had done with his time here so far. Or if he was like me, kind of lonely when it came to other humans, and still looking for a way through.

I was about to turn fifty, and had started experiencing a strange kind of dysphoria, not of gender—that was nothing new—but more of age. I remembered being a young child watching my grandmother put on her face powder, looking at herself in the gold-rimmed bathroom mirror. She was so alive—the most alive person I've ever known. I always watched her closely. She was talking to me that day, but mostly talking to herself, explaining how disorienting it was to look in a mirror.

"I still feel like I'm twenty-five," she'd said. "I'm not totally sure how this happened."

She patted her face gently and smiled down at me. She was in her seventies at the time. I wished she was still here so we could talk, now that I understand all too well exactly what she'd meant.

When I looked in the mirror, I could see all my younger selves: they were right there, so close to the surface, but I wasn't sure at all what other people saw when they looked at me. Jude, for example. She is about ten years younger, without a wrinkle somehow, and her smooth face always glows a warm brown the minute the sun comes out. I wondered what she saw when she looked at me, which she did. Sometimes I caught her eyes lingering on me just a catch too long—at friends' dinner parties, at the post office or at the grocery store—and my stomach fluttered ridiculously. Those lingering moments made me dizzy with a disorienting ache. But which version of me was she seeing?

More than seeing my younger selves, I wanted her to see what was underneath all that, that part of me that's hidden deep in the center of my body, layered over with muscle and bone and sinew and skin. In an Eastern Philosophy class I took in college, we learned about the koshas—that the innermost one is the hardest to access, tucked away underneath the veils of the body, the nervous system, and even consciousness. I guess I wanted her to see that deepest part, even if I couldn't often see it myself.

Maybe I should have just summoned my courage to ask what she felt about me. I didn't have anything to lose—maybe just my dignity, which, if I was being honest, had never been worth much.

An enormous seagull swooped overhead and landed on the wet sand nearby, pecking at a dead crab and eyeing me. He was beautiful with a robust, shimmering body and dark pink feet. He looked like he'd just been to the salon, so put together. Poor seagulls, they are relentlessly underappreciated creatures. He moved closer to me, stepped from side to side, and I understood he was trying to give me a message. I asked him if he comes here often, told him he was a total babe. He already knew it. He ruffled his feathers and puffed up even bigger. A show off. I could have a crush on this bird, I thought.

Once I met a different seagull who I'm sure was Victor. Same eyes somehow. I asked him to tell me what had happened in that hotel room all those years ago. If it was an accident or not. When they found his body, it was twisted sickeningly with rigor mortis, face down on the yellow bathroom tiles. Accidental overdose of fentanyl, the police report said. I didn't even know he had been into those kinds of drugs. I was under the impression when he died that he still shared everything with me, and finding out he didn't was another layer of loss.

In the distance, I could see that the alien family had started packing up their chairs. Bianca looked cold now, rubbing her bare arms to warm herself. The father had not moved the whole time, just sat there looking like a grim baked potato, but he was in motion now, dragging the chairs behind him up the embankment, leaving strange tracks in the sand. The little brother brought up the rear, covered in muck from head to toe. He stopped and turned around to look right back at me. He raised both middle fingers from his tiny fists to flip me off, maybe as a final alien test to see how I'd respond. I gave him a little salute before he turned to catch up.

The sky was getting heavier and the wind had picked up. Behind me was a thick stand of forest wilderness that stretches for miles. No one ever goes in there; everyone just wants the beach.

I closed my eyes for a moment, enjoying the sound of the waves crashing. I could smell there was a storm brewing.

As the wind picked up, I looked behind me at the forest where I knew I would be more protected from the elements—I wasn't ready to go home yet. I walked towards that dark stand of trees and they welcomed me easily. I picked my way along a narrow deer trail, jumped across a small creek, and crawled over two downed trees, rotting and covered with mushrooms. About a mile in, I was at the enormous rock that looks like a sea lion's head, where a hundred thousand years ago he flopped out of the sea and never left, decided to be stone instead. I read somewhere that sea lions are descendants of a bear-like terrestrial, so it makes sense he would be here, out of the salty depths and back to the trees where it all started.

I had been visiting this spot for years, drawn to it most strongly when melancholy threatened to overtake me. I always found solace there and this day was no different. I sat down and leaned against the sea lion bear and patted his shiny nose while the wet moss beneath me seeped moisture into my jeans. No bother.

I laid all the way down, with the moss as a pillow, and started having a fantasy about Jude. Not an unusual occurrence, but this one felt different, like maybe it could actually happen.

In my fantasy I imagined that just once a year, maybe in early September when the air here is the warmest, we would agree to meet in this place, hidden in the thick trees. We would have a pact not to tell anyone, regardless of if we were dating other people, and never to talk about it together before or after. We would meet there at sunset and probably not say anything. Maybe we would kiss—I hoped we would. Maybe we would smell that secret smell that lives low on the neck. Maybe we would take our clothes off and lay close against each other on a bed of redwood needles. We would be together in this different way to really try to see who we each were underneath all the skin and bone, to the innermost hidden kosha that needs so many layers of protection.

When I opened my eyes the sky was dark, but there was still a bit of fading light coming through the trees. I brushed myself off, gave the sea lion bear a pat, and headed out.

When I made it back to the beach, the sun was setting behind thick clouds on the horizon and the darkening sky was saturated with burnt orange. I started making my way back towards the river trail that would take me home.

In the distance ahead of me was a lone figure—a silhouetted body I had memorized a thousand times, rabbit-smooth and vital. She waved and called my name—started walking directly to where I stood.

I waited there for her with the trees at my back and the ocean before me—humming with all my energy—alive, alive, alive.

Those Coyote Teeth

Tonight Jada gets my attention when she throws back a shot of mezcal and then says to the crowd gathered at the gallery's bar that the best part of her last one-night stand was using a cucumber as a dildo.

Jada is married to a man named Jeffrey and their two-year-old son is also named Jeffrey. We've all met before at other art openings, the occasional party, and once chatted in the shade of a maple tree at the farmer's market, but never had more to say than the most basic of social niceties. *How's the baby doing? When is the next art opening?* that kind of thing. What I've noticed at these run-ins is that all three of them enjoy being the center of attention and that the Jeffreys often let their round, pale bellies poke out of their designer t-shirts. I assume Jada's one-night stand happened before the Jeffreys but know it is best not to make such assumptions.

Only little Jeffrey accompanies Jada this evening. As I turn away from the bar, he yells out "Dildo!" from where he is perched on Jada's hip and everyone laughs. He beams out at us like a comedic savant and claps his hands together. His fat, little baby legs remind me of the spicy sausages I couldn't stop eating the last time I went to Sicily.

My girlfriend Claire comes over to find out what all the

commotion is about. She is the university gallery's new director and spent months putting this show together. Claire is one of those extroverts who can remember names, faces, interesting anecdotes, and every tedious detail of what people like and dislike about a piece of art, which is how she landed this coveted gallery position. The art opening tonight is a series of paintings from a Canadian artist who lives on Vancouver Island. They are huge, floor to ceiling, with a lot of rounded shapes and warm colors: oranges, browns, soft greens. Each one of them looks like a place I would like to climb into and have a good rest.

Claire kisses me on the cheek, squeezes my hand, and smiles at Jada and little Jeffrey before heading back to the main floor. She knows I'll probably go back to our apartment soon; we learned early on in our dating that we are perhaps not the most socially compatible couple. I like going out, getting drinks, and dancing on occasion, but am always ready to leave many hours before Claire. She prefers to be the last one standing at any given event and usually is.

Tonight when she comes home after closing up the gallery and getting one last drink with the artist and a few friends. She crawls into bed smelling of whiskey and asks, "Do you think it's weird that Jeffrey wasn't there tonight?"

"Not really. Guess he couldn't make it," I say.

I make my voice sound uninterested, but when I roll over I can't sleep for another two hours after Claire passes out, wondering not why Jeffrey wasn't there, but why Claire noticed.

I stare at the ceiling and start thinking about how I came out at fourteen.

When I looked at page after page of penises in the *Playgirl* magazines my best friend Jenine stole from her aunt, all I could think of were weasels, desperate for some weasel thing beyond my comprehension.

"People, like, want to touch these things?" I'd asked Jenine, who gave me a funny look before nodding. She said she thought they were pretty hot herself and told me that her cousin Sarah had even licked one once.

A few weeks later, as my mom drove me to the orthodontist to get my braces tightened, I fiddled with my seatbelt and blurted out, "I'm definitely GAY." It came out in a nervous rush, but I felt lighter immediately. My mom kept her hands on the wheel and her eyes on the road.

"Maxine, just please don't be the kind of homosexual that feels the need to be naked in a parade," she responded before turning into the parking lot and telling me to get an extra free toothbrush for her. "Your bare ass won't ever look as good in the hot sun as you think it will, trust me."

Sometimes I think Claire and I will be together forever, and sometimes I think it's a miracle we've lasted the past three years. We met at a bar, both there on other dates that weren't going great. I couldn't take my eyes off her—her sturdy frame, short messy hair, and a laugh that cut through everything—even from across the room. We exchanged numbers in the bathroom. Up close she was even more attractive, with lines starting to emerge around her eyes from smiling, from sun, from life. That was kind of it—we broke things off with the people we had been seeing and went on our first date the next week.

We get along well, have enough varied interests that we usually have something compelling to talk about together. Sex during our first few years together was overwhelming and glorious. That has faded, but it's still satisfying. Everyone says we are great together and we've always agreed.

All this being true, I find myself getting lost in daydreams a lot lately—of spending the rest of my thirties alone in the Cascade Mountains somewhere, eating cans of cold refried beans and making all my clothing out of fern fronds, whereas Claire gets nervous if we are away from the city for more than a day.

This is not to say I'm antisocial. I think maybe I just read the Transcendentalists at too formative a moment—self-reliance and all that: Thoreau in the woods and Emerson seeing God in the leaves and branches. There are many humans I love to be around. Okay, maybe not *many*, but I think I'm pretty normal. I am decent at making conversation, have a couple close friends I've known for years, and I go out with my coworkers most Fridays after work—normal stuff.

Claire increasingly talks about wanting kids, but even just the idea of parenthood is an onslaught to my senses. Little Jeffrey is adorable but not adorable enough for me to go through with having one of my own. Even as a child, when I first learned where babies come from—and how they come out—I was certain that would not be something I'd be participating in. I love spending time with my friends' kids and I also really enjoy it when, at the end of our fun time together, they go back to their own house. I think of myself as more of a future honorary aunt/uncle: Auncle Max has a nice, unique ring to it.

Many years ago in college, during one of our regular office hour meetings, my wildlife ecology professor shared with me—in an ashamed, desperate whisper like she had just accidentally shat in the pool—that deciding to be a parent was her biggest regret. Since then, no one besides her has admitted it out loud, but when I look around, I see that my friends and acquaintances who once partook in relatively easy existences can now be found crying quietly in the bathroom with bloodshot eyes and goo on their shirts. They start fixating on the probability of terrible things happening and become prone to perseveration, worried for their wunderkind that at any moment in the near or distant future there could be bullying, drug issues, dismemberment, disease, and death. Even the emergence of a dumb, lazy, or ill-tempered personality in their child would be its own kind of tragedy. Their beautiful baby could turn into a chauvinist incel or a shut-in conspiracy theorist with a basement full of guns from Walmart. In the bright light of day though, most people say becoming a parent was *the best thing that ever happened to them*. I just don't think I can do it.

If Claire decides parenthood is what she wants, that will most likely be the end of us. This is probably the main source of my ambivalence about our relationship, even when things are going well. She'll probably go on to marry some well-adjusted, esteemed, professional type with inherited family money who really wants kids. She and I won't talk for years, but eventually we will make a kind of real peace and keep in touch with life's highlights. I'll become that estranged but friendly auncle who sends birthday cards with a crisp twenty-dollar bill from somewhere far away.

I'm a little surprised when Jada texts to see if I want to grab coffee over the weekend. Claire drove up to Portland to attend a conference for the week and I'm shocked at how quickly I reverted to a kind of easy bachelorhood. There have been recordlong showers, lazy midday masturbations, and eating cold pizza for dinner with a sense of profound contentment.

Jada and I decide to meet at The Filling Station, a cafe near the university packed with bright, young adults who make me feel both geriatric and profoundly grateful to not still be in my early twenties. She gives me a big hug like we are old friends when I walk in but then suddenly seems nervous, twisting her hair around her finger while her eyes dart around. We talk about little Jeffrey's nap schedule, how she is getting back into making art while he sleeps. And she mentions Jeffrey Sr. being away a lot.

"The thing is," she tells me after an awkward silence, her face so lean and sad, "I just don't know how I ended up here, with this life. It feels very strange sometimes."

"Yeah, I get that," I respond, holding her gaze as my eyes well up, but not knowing what else to say.

I want to tell her the truth, that I don't know how I ended up here either. I worry about what that means for Claire and me when—until very recently—it's seemed as though we were so right together. I'm not ready for my recent worries to be laid on the table and spilled on by lukewarm cappuccinos, so I don't say anything.

"Do you and Claire want kids?" she asks, reading my mind.

I look at the wall behind Jada. There is a poster of Janis Joplin in tight bell bottoms, screaming into the microphone, all raw passion with her famous line printed across the middle: *on stage I make love to twenty-five thousand different people, and then I go home alone.*

I think about how to answer Jada's question.

"Claire wants kids but I really don't. I like how my life is. Well, that might be stretching it a bit." We both laugh more easily now. "I just don't think having a kid is a good idea for me. It sounds unbearably disruptive to the life I want to build. Sorry to say it. That's probably not very helpful."

"Actually it is helpful—it's very honest. You're not trying to convince me of anything. When people try to tell me all this is normal and these parental and relationship doubts will pass, I second-guess myself even more. I think I actually feel better right now than I have in a while."

We look at each other for a second too long. I want to ask her something but get distracted by her long eyelashes and the downy fuzz on her cheeks I've never noticed before.

I look down at the table and then back at her. "This is a weird question, but do you ever think of yourself as a portal? Like, really, isn't it so weird that a human can come out of another human? It's like all the special people with uteruses helped everyone who is here on Earth come through from the other side."

I look at her open face, feel my cheeks reddening. "Sorry," I say into this new silence, "I guess I've just been thinking about portals lately."

She is looking at me so seriously but then she laughs, and that's when I first see her coyote teeth. She puts her hand over her mouth instinctively; I hope not from anything she saw in my reaction. It is alarming though, all those white, pointy knives long and gleaming with gaps in between. Almost like normal teeth, but not. I wonder how I've never noticed before, because she laughs often, makes jokes. I remember a few years ago, my mom told me that when I was born, she got a strange mole on her face, and also in that year the texture of her skin changed, her feet sloughing off layers for no reason. Apparently, these types of unexpected changes are part of procreation. Maybe Jada's teeth were something like that.

"I can honestly say I've never thought of it like that before," she says, settling herself after my question. "I really don't know why I'm laughing," she says. "Maybe that explains everything: the truth is I was a portal and now I'm just very tired."

There's silence again but it's comfortable now. She looks at the clock and gives me a half-smile. She seems a little less sad.

"Thanks for meeting up with me, Max. I really needed this. You know, I've wanted to be friends with you for a while now."

I smile back, feeling better than I did earlier, but there's another feeling too that I can't place. We get up, hug goodbye. She walks back to her car and I watch her go—her lithe, canine body moving easily amongst the other, regular pedestrians. I feel both lightheaded and at a loss, and realize I just want to be outside, alone. This happens to me sometimes when I get a rush of feeling, especially a feeling I don't understand.

There's a place in the woods just outside of town I go to often. It's about a thirty-minute drive to the trailhead. The trail winds along a creek and down to a lake they stock with trout. There's a rocky outcropping on the other side, far away from the little roped-off beach where people take their kids to splash around in the shallows. There's an unmarked, overgrown deer trail that leads to a cave if you know where to look.

Sometimes, like now, when I feel overwhelmed but don't know exactly why, I make my way there. It's a relief that close enough to downtown there's still real wilderness nearby. I have the sense that if I hid out there it would take people days, maybe weeks, to find me. Sometimes, if I'm having anxiety, I sit in the cave and feel worse, imagining a big earthquake finally hitting and dislodging hundreds of tons of dark rock onto my body and the crushing and cracking and dust that would settle. But usually I feel better.

I keep thinking about Jada's crazy teeth. I wonder if Claire has noticed them. I wonder if when Jeffrey Jr. gets his adult teeth if they'll be all wild and pointy too. I wonder if her canine smile turns Jeffrey Sr. on, makes him even harder than that one-night stand cucumber. My mind sees Jenine's hand flip to a page in one of her magazines with an extra huge weasel penis, and I wonder what happened to her after high school.

I lay back on the rocks where there's an indentation that fits my body perfectly, stare at the dark, wet ceiling, and cry for no apparent reason, or for all the reasons, until I feel like myself again and head back towards home.

When Claire gets back from Portland, a day later than expected, something is off. I can't tell if it's her or if it's me. I let a couple more days go by, hoping it will pass. It doesn't.

"I have to tell you something," Claire says while I'm getting out the cream for our morning coffee. "I know you don't want kids, but I'm ready. I finally have the job I've been working towards for so long and I feel excited for what's next. And I don't want to use a sperm bank; I want Jeffrey to be the sperm donor. I already asked him about it and he said yes."

"You talked to him before you talked to me?" I ask, setting my empty mug down on the counter and looking at her more carefully. "When did this happen?"

"We were both in Portland last week and met up," she says, avoiding eye contact.

"Does Jada know about this?" I ask.

"He's telling her this morning," Claire says. "I know this all probably sounds like it's out of nowhere and reckless, but I've thought a lot about it and it feels right to me."

"Wait," I say, figuring it out, "you guys...hooked up in Portland?"

A nauseating wave churns in my stomach—what I imagine

morning sickness must feel like.

For some reason I start thinking back to the wildlife ecology class I took with that professor. She told us about how coyotes are monogamous, but how well-adapted they are to change. I remember something about how they rarely make their own dens and instead just move into abandoned ones. I think about Jada and her coyote teeth, how razor-sharp they are, and imagine them tearing her house to unrecognizable shreds when she finds out about all this. I imagine Claire and Jeffrey in some fancy hotel room, and the thing is, it actually kind of makes sense. It dawns on me that I feel more relieved than angry, though I don't want Claire to know this yet. I give her my evilest eye, throw some stuff in a bag, and don't say another word.

It's a cold, foggy day so there are no swimmers at the lake. The quiet hovers over the water like a blanket and back at the cave it is even quieter. I sit down in my usual spot, lean back and close my eyes, thinking about portals, and where this one might take me. The wind is picking up and rustling through the trees, a hawk lets out a piercing shriek over the water, and the sun is starting to burn through the fog high in the sky, sharpening everything. There are no long shadows yet.

I have the idea of asking Jada if she and little Jeffrey would want to come up to the lake to swim sometime when it's warmer, imagine the baby's sturdy legs kicking the water with delight, and then inviting them to my cave—the three of us just lying there together in the dark quiet—not like in a coyote den, not forever, just for a long, still moment, pretending we're home.

I Am a Conservationist

Georgie is twelve and doesn't give a fuck. His tantrums extended from the terrible twos and I stopped counting when I realized it only depressed me further to keep track of how long this has gone on, becoming clear that it wasn't a phase but a personality.

Other dads I know see me at the grocery store and when I tell them how I'm struggling, they like to remind me of those preschool co-op days when all the parents took shifts for daycare and Georgie would stand in the corner, look unflinchingly into the eyes of whoever was in the room and slowly shit his pants. They think it's hilarious.

There's this one dad from the co-op, Gabe, who is completely gorgeous, I have to admit. His whole family is gorgeous. His wife is tall with curly black hair, and she has shown up in my dreams more than once. Their kids are perfectly put together, I mean, they get good grades, and do extracurricular activities people actually admire, like kung fu and tennis. They like to exert themselves, feel their hearts pumping, that kind of thing. They look like they've been raised on organic cream and fresh strawberries their whole lives. Those tan, rosy-cheeked complexions. And their twinkly-eyed smiles that seem so genuine. My god.

My wife says it's no good to compare one's insides to other

people's outsides. You can never know what another person or family is actually like, regardless of what you see on the surface, at a party or a PTA meeting. I know she's right, but I can't help feeling we got it all wrong. Really wrong.

Samuel is our other kid though. He's younger than Georgie and has a relaxed air about him, moving through the world with a lopsided grin. He'll be fine, I know that. Nothing sticks to him. He's like water in a creek, everything tumbling away, easy.

Once when Samuel was two and Georgie was four, we sat in our backyard under this ancient oak tree. To be honest, that tree was the main reason I wanted to scrape the money together to buy this ramshackle house on the coast. I am a conservationist at my core and couldn't bear the thought of rich assholes buying this place and taking down the tree.

Anyways, I was in the yard blowing bubbles for the kids. It was one of those unusually warm spring days you know can't last, and everything was new, bright, and green, all the fresh buds and small leaves emerging. Samuel was giggling his hearty baby laugh, sitting there like a little fatso, all wobbly and perfectly alive. The bubbles would float over and his face would light up even more. It was one of those impossibly cute things you see your own kid doing and think for a split second you're part of something worthwhile after all. But then slowly pan the camera over and you'll see Georgie stiff-faced, digging his filthy little hands into the spring dirt, coming up with mud and pebbles, looking me in the eye as he shoves it all in his mouth.

With that unflinching stare, he tears up grass roots and a little worm writhes in his grip. I know this isn't too abnormal or anything. Kid stuff, right? But I can't take my eyes away from his eyes and I'm frozen like a damn idiot. I guess most parents would pull the kid's hands out of his mouth, wipe them off and with a little laugh, *Why are you eating dirt, silly?* But I don't do that. I keep watching him, still like a statue. I let him eat the dirt and rocks. I imagine them solidifying in his throat and stomach like clay, turning him back into earth, his whole heavy body sinking down into the soil, far, far away from us. In that moment, in the deepest part of myself, I know for certain that if Samuel's joyous laughter is a part of me, Georgie's darkness absolutely is also, maybe even more so.

I look up into the oak tree, its knobby arms reaching out in all directions, like the arthritic fingers of a wise geriatric, craggy with age. I wonder if the tree has observed my parenting and what it thinks about the state of things and what other moments it has observed in its hundreds of years here and if the tree thinks this moment of ours, of mine, is the worst. I don't remember cleaning Georgie off, but I must have. We must have gone inside and I must have made the kids something to eat. Maybe we read a story, maybe they took a nap. Maybe I felt terrified for the future and maybe I felt like other fathers surely must feel: responsible, but unfathomably weary. Missing something important, something innate I can't seem to access in spite of the parenting books I pore over, the community forums I visit online late at night when I can't sleep, or the hours with my therapist (who is also raising sons, although seemingly more successfully). *Don't compare yourself to your therapist!* my wife says. I know she's right, but I don't know how to stop.

Here's twelve-year-old Georgie coming through the front door now, looking pissed. He's got the wild-eyed look of a caged animal. I say hi but he doesn't say hi back. He grimaces like a rabid wolverine, the front teeth he refuses to brush are yellowed already like those of a hardened tobacco smoker. He's slamming his backpack down at the entrance to the house where we've asked him not to leave it a thousand times, and heading for his video games where he can shoot and kill with abandon. He's an angry, old, drunk in a skinny, prepubescent body, weaving around the room, knocking things over.

I want to grab him and shake him hard until he snaps out of it, shake him as hard as I can until he becomes reasonable, shake him until he turns eighteen and understands things better, or at least gets out of our house to go off and ruin relationships with other people I don't know, but now that I think about it, feel like I should warn: *Be careful. He'll take you down with him.*

But it's too late for anything a good shake could accomplish. I can't admit it out loud to my wife, but even she must know somewhere deep inside herself I gave up on him turning out alright many years ago. A good shake won't help any of us. It's far too late for that.

The Wind

Things started getting strange in the town of Looking, Oregon in spring, when the north winds began howling. Hundred-year-old evergreen trees, stout-trunked and towering, swayed like saplings. The dark green river that ran right past city hall had whitecaps that splashed up to the crumbling sidewalk, and Johnny, the unlikely future valedictorian of his class of seven students at Driftwood High School (their mascot was a hunk of wood that got dressed in a jersey for football games), started trying to figure out how he could surf it on an old board his father had left behind. Johnny spent a lot of his time on the internet, not even with games like his friends, blowing things up, but gathering information. He was a sweet boy with a gap between his teeth and very small ears that he used to hold back his black, silky hair. He told anyone who would listen that when he graduated, he was going to get a tattoo of the American flag across his whole back. Almost everyone he knew thought it was a great idea; they felt reassured by it even if they didn't know why.

Only Hellie asked him, "What does that actually mean to you?" but he didn't understand her question or how to answer.

The last time Johnny had seen him, his father had been almost handsome but jumpy (the drugs, the drugs, the drugs). His teeth were starting to crumble—and that had been a few years ago now.

"Can't you take me with you to wherever you're going?" Johnny had asked him, but his dad had only clenched his jaw and changed the subject.

At the grocery store, Esther, wearing a faded, blue house dress three sizes too large, announced that the wind had blown every single blossom off her apple tree. She rubbed her temples while Lennie, the cashier, nodded and sighed and tried to move her through the line. Esther counted her change slowly for the loaf of bread she was buying and cleared her throat.

"My apple tree had never had this many blossoms on it and now because of this goddamn wind they're all rotting on the ground," she said, looking like she might cry or punch something or someone in her despair.

Someone in the back of the line chimed in. "It's part of climate collapse. Well, probably." Lennie took a deep breath and knew if Esther started crying or trying to fight someone, he would never get everyone through the checkout line before closing. On top of that there would probably be someone's soft serve dripping onto the floor just like Esther's tears and at least one tantruming toddler, too tired to be civilized, who Lenny would find relatable.

Johnny hadn't told anyone except Marcos, the sheriff, that he had found a human femur on the beach the day before. He imagined asking Lennie to make an announcement over the loudspeaker telling everyone everything, including that Johnny wasn't sure at first that it was human. He had carried it home and looked it up online. Marcos had confirmed. Johnny wanted to look out upon his neighbors' faces when they heard the news, imagined watching their eyes light up with surprise, then seeing their eyebrows crease with the next wave of *I wonder who it is*, but Marcos had told him he was opening an investigation and to not say anything to anyone.

Esther's eightieth birthday was coming up in September. She waddled through town like a llama escaped from its pasture, all scraggly neck and big, yellow teeth, spitting in your face for any perceived slight. Esther was hard to like but easier to love. She didn't have friends exactly, but when she twisted her ankle the year before, people brought meals over for almost three months, plus elaborate desserts and the kind of wine she liked best: a boxed cabernet sold at Thompson's for four dollars on extended sale. Several neighbors had already added special ingredients to their shopping lists.

Esther was a fretter, a forehead rubber, and a gossip. She had long, thinning hair she tied up in a tight, scraggly bun that the wind was working on letting loose. While she moved on from the topic of her apple tree to share her fears about the fate of her new windsock in the gales that kept blasting, Lennie looked past her out the window, watched an osprey fly past with a fish in its claws, and wished he was outside, even in the terrible wind—anywhere but working the checkout line.

The only person Esther didn't irritate was Johnny (Johnny James)—the secret bone-finder—who everyone called JJ, which he hated, or Johnny Jimmy, which made him feel murderous. He would have preferred to be called Jonathan James Duncan III or maybe Jonathan J. Duncan Esq., but no one would take him seriously. He was fifteen and nobody listened. Sometimes when it was too rainy, or too windy, or just too awful for any other number of reasons (angry bullies, angry dogs, angry mother), Johnny would knock on Esther's front door and she would invite him in for something sweet to eat.

"You're back?" she asked him every time she let him in. Johnny wasn't sure if she was glad or disappointed to find him there.

"One thing I can tell you," she said as the door closed behind him, "is I actually like when people gossip about me. I like to hear what they come up with!" She laughed to herself, remembering. "Once someone said I got impregnated by a pirate...when I was fifty-nine! The rumor was I'd been seen fornicating with him in the early morning hours, right out on the beach below the Castaway. That I had a baby that looked like a seal. Supposedly, it died in the cold air and I threw it into the ocean off the dock."

Esther liked to talk about people in town, what they did and didn't do, who was having an affair with who, who was drinking too much, who was spreading rumors about ex-lovers at parties where people were high on various things, hungry for fresh dirt because they were bored with their own lives and relationships. She liked to talk about, for instance, who stole all the wind chimes off of the awning at City Hall last summer when the mayor was still halfheartedly trying to spruce things up a bit. Esther explained to Johnny that the mayor was having a midlife crisis and had developed feelings for a married woman in town. The married woman had submitted a couple ideas to the suggestion box and the mayor had never been so eager to initiate a project. And it was true that Johnny had seen the mayor out in front of the building with a paintbrush, putting another coat of paint on the peeling window trim.

Lately Esther had been talking about how someone in town had been putting their extra zucchini (that absolutely no one wanted) in their neighbors' cars at night when everyone was asleep. People would go to warm their engines up in the morning and find an enormous, green phallus sitting upright like a small child, seatbelt and all.

Johnny was fine to listen and he also would have been fine if she didn't say anything at all and they just sat there and looked out the window in silence. He didn't want to go home, didn't want to play football, soccer, or cross country after school, didn't want to go to the library, didn't want to do weight training at the school gym, didn't want to race dirt bikes, didn't want to talk about cars, how fast and expensive they were or how to fix them up, and didn't want to get a girlfriend.

He did still want a tattoo of an American flag on his back even though he wasn't sure he could articulate why. As far as he could tell, these were his only options in Looking. Going to Esther's house didn't make sense either, but he kept finding himself on her porch, his knuckles rapping against that thick, old door. He couldn't explain it but didn't have to because no one was asking.

"What I really wanted when I was young," Esther told Johnny once, "was to be a philosopher. Like Simone de Beauvoir. Simone had a lot of wild ideas...and lovers," she said, and smiled so wide he could see all her gold fillings in the back. He made a note to look up who this Simone was when he had a chance.

Daniel Holcomb went to Thompson's for a very short list of groceries: beer, aspirin, bananas, chocolate chips, and toilet paper. He foraged, grew, or made everything else he and his daughter needed. He could have made the beer too, but he didn't have the patience for fermentation; though he was fine making butter and cheese himself, using and reusing old cheesecloth and scraped rennet. He saw the forest around him as a tree farm to be harvested from, and had logged almost everything but the dogwood planted in the front yard when his daughter Hellie had been brought home from the hospital. She was born early, flying into the nurse's waiting arms at a lean five pounds. He liked to imagine her flying, but in actuality she was pulled out in a whirlwind of crisis. She weighed exactly as much as a $1.99 bag of potatoes from Thompson's. She was so small. The dogwood was a gift from their neighbor, a retired arborist.

"Plant it in a place you can see easily from the house," she'd said. "Watch the tree and your daughter grow together. I'm so sorry about your loss."

Hellie's mother had died in labor. Preeclampsia. Sonya had been in perfect health, supposedly had "perfect hips for child-bearing." Several women in town had said she seemed to have been "born to birth," which made Sonya furious. Daniel wondered if this was her way of proving them wrong—to show them that her body was not actually made for making babies at all, but for some other special purpose they couldn't fathom.

Daniel had named his daughter, sitting by the fire with her in a rocking chair, several weeks after Sonya's death. He knew his wife would have questioned his choice. They hadn't talked about names before; they were going to wait to meet her first.

"Hellie?! Like the Hell's Angels? Really, Dan," he could imagine her saying, "she's just a baby."

He had named her Hellie because he thought it might make her tougher. Hellion, Hellraiser, Hellie. She was such a tiny creature. He was scared to be alone with her at first, but he forced himself to figure it out. And he had, more or less.

Hellie was too young to remember this but they had buried Sonya at sea, put her body out into the Pacific after much paperwork was submitted to the Navy and Marine Corps Mortuary Affairs Office. It had been solemn and they both had gotten seasick. He didn't like to think about it, wondering if he should have just buried her on land so Hellie could visit her grave properly—not just leave her to stare at the vastness of the ocean and wonder where she was. Nothing he had done felt right.

Daniel was a quiet man, slow to anger, except when he thought people were acting the fool—he couldn't tolerate that at all. Not in his line of work, away in the forest, no cell service, felling trees with young men wielding chainsaws who already started off a little on the wild side. Any false move could mean death. Because of this, even away from work, he found any variety of clowning or jackassery intolerable.

The spring winds made him and his whole crew nervous. Accidents happened in the wind and the wind would not stop howling. It had been months since the last still day with no breeze. At the bar after work, someone said he'd seen a wooden picnic table blow down the road like it was nothing. "It was airborne," the man had said, "floating across the sky like a balloon."

The woman who owned the pizza shop said the business sign—heavy steel she had welded herself—had blown away and vanished. The bartender, not known to ever have lied, shared that his neighbor's toddler had rolled down the road like a ball of yarn, but not to worry—little Henry was fine, just two scraped elbows and some lingering dizziness. Almost everyone went to the bar that spring, sometimes twice a day. It was a place to escape. The wind was that bad.

Lennie hated beer so he always got a shot of bourbon—neat—even though what he truly liked were the sweet, too-colorful cocktails made from vodka and fruity soda that young women barely of drinking age always seemed to order when he used to go out to the nicer bars in Portland. He sometimes made one for himself in the privacy of his own kitchen, added a little umbrella if he was in a particular mood, but even in his own home he felt embarrassed and would drink it quickly, praying that no one would stop by.

Lennie thought about time and space, how nothing was linear, everything vast. It seemed impossible that fifteen years ago was when he first landed in Looking. He had been with his boyfriend Matthew then, and they had a fight—more like a reckoning—they couldn't recover from. Lennie didn't even remember what the conversation had originally been about, just that Matthew had cried out in anguish and then said in a hoarse whisper, "It's like you just punched me in the face and now you're telling me how bad your hand hurts." He was sobbing into his own hands. "Fucking go to hell, Lennie." It was a lie Lennie told himself that he didn't remember. He remembered. He wished he didn't.

Two ravens sit near each other on the roof of the mortuary, cackling to themselves. Rain is about to downpour, but at the moment there's just a light drizzle. The birds ruffle their feathers in unison, nuzzle each other. One has a shiny bead he stole from a necklace someone lost on the trail to the lake, and the other has a long finger held together in one piece by stubborn ligaments. She pecks at the bits of cartilage still attached in the middle, wanting to wave it around and cause a scene.

Daniel didn't say much at the bar that afternoon, just drank his neat glass of scotch and listened. He thought of Sonya and how he still missed her. (The wind rattled the dirty windows.) He mulled over the times he had not been as kind as he should have been, and the times he had not taken her seriously. (The wind knocked something off the outside of the door.) He couldn't think of a time he'd offered to do the dishes or rub her tired feet. He had a hard time thinking of anything selfless he had done: it seemed that everything he'd done for her was something that benefited him. (The wind came in under the door and swirled around some boot dust.) He tried to let these thoughts go, knowing he couldn't do anything about any of it now. She was long gone, but also not. He let himself remember how she used to blow her hair out of her eyes instead of just pushing it to the side with a hand. It was these little things he remembered that cut him to the quick.

He had not made the same mistakes with Hellie. He listened to her and thanked her when she was helpful, even when she was very much not helpful but was trying to be. He noticed and commented with genuine attentiveness and curiosity on things she shared with him, and told her she was smart and beautiful and too good for this town.

He still made mistakes but loved her as well as he could, reminded himself when he was tired and grumpy or lonely or angry or scared that none of that was her fault, and none of it had been Sonya's fault either: it just took him too long to figure that out for himself and he was sorry. He looked down into the dark, potent liquid before him as the conversation in the bar shifted from wind to the fact that the almanac said the upcoming summer would be shorter than usual. He thought of that one October Sonya had asked him—begged him, though it was not in her nature to beg—to take her somewhere to see the fall leaves change in their full splendor, away from all these incessant evergreens. And maybe to some hot springs she had read about online. He had told her that he couldn't get away. It hadn't been the truth and he realized she had never asked him for anything like that again.

He closed his eyes as the jukebox started playing an old Fleetwood Mac song and tried to think of any possible reason he could have had to refuse her. He couldn't think of a single one. He had stopped trying to make her happy, as he had in the beginning, but wasn't sure why or what had changed to make it this way. He pictured Sonya so clearly in his mind, like he was conjuring her, and said to her without moving his lips: *I'm so sorry, I'm so sorry, I'm so sorry.*

Hellie spent her childhood in the passenger seat of her father's enormous truck, reading poetry books from the library while he loaded up the dead bodies of very old trees and yelled at the men on his crew to not be idiots. She was fourteen and still sat next to him on the worn bench seat, looking at the books on her lap, which she loved, but was really focused on something else.

When she looked out the window, she chanted under her breath, "Stay away, babies. Stay away, babies. Stay away, babies," to keep the deer away, to keep the opossums away, and to keep everyone else (all the other creatures, The Little People, she called them) away too.

For deer and elk (and bears, of course), her father would swerve, but smaller animals did not change his course. She always thought he was cruel, maybe even a psychopath (once she had learned that word), then realized on a rainy day, just last spring, that it was for her safety that he tried never to veer off course. If she even thought about the thumping feel of an animal under her father's truck, she would get dizzy and throw up, so she told the animals over and over to stay away with her mind, to wait, to listen, to not come until the road was clear. She looked ahead at the dark trees on either side of the road as they drove and made an invisible wall with her mind to keep the animals back until it was safe to cross. When she focused, it worked, but she worried a millisecond of lost vigilance could be the worst kind of failure: death to an innocent. She had to concentrate more intently and keep at it. She would not be able to forgive herself if she let her attention falter.

Hellie herself was not afraid to die. She was a student of death. Sometimes she imagined starting her own school called The School of Death. People would find it strange at first, but it would be very beautiful, and with time they would see that. She wondered if there was a way to study death in college but didn't feel comfortable asking any adults she knew. They wouldn't actually listen to her ideas but think she needed therapeutic help because her mother had died.

A few times, she had turned around after her father didn't swerve to watch creatures struggle to make their last movements, or not. She had watched squirming bees be pulled apart by ants and seen great Douglas fir trees turn skeletal with beetle infestations, becoming a whole forest of ghosts.

Sometimes lives went quickly though and she was glad for that. She wanted to go quickly too—she knew that already. She once told Lennie this, when she was in first grade and getting herself some gummy bears at Thompson's (sneakily, because Daniel was such a purist and he could not/would not make gummy bears), but Lennie had been so overwhelmed with his own anxieties that he didn't take the time he wished he would have to listen to her. Lennie knew that Hellie would die for any animal. Even in his distraction he remembered that was what she had been trying to explain. If she could be assured no more trucks would hit any more animals, she would die right there on the spot, no questions asked. On bad days, the darkest days, her chant went from *stay away, babies*, to *take me instead*, something she wouldn't confess to anyone until she was in her early twenties and tipsy for the first time at a party in Portland.

In elementary school, Hellie was put into remedial math classes. While her classmates clamored to recite their multiplication tables, Hellie sat quietly and took note of each person's body language and what it meant, calculated the distance between her own eyes and the tree out the window in feet, then inches. When she learned about centimeters, she did that calculation as well. She measured the space between the bodies of Johnny and Zeke, who almost always maintained a distance of three feet (91.44 centimeters) from each other, with no eye contact and frequent insults. She had known them her whole life and they pretended to hate each other, but once in a rainstorm, she'd seen them kissing against a tree.

Hellie determined the height and width of the glass windows that looked out onto the basketball courts and the forest beyond, and estimated (correctly) how many buckets of shards they would hold if shattered by the tsunami that everyone said was inevitable.

His dad long gone, Johnny's mother called him only "Dipshit" as in "Dipshit, you peed on the toilet seat" (he didn't) and "Dipshit, where are my car keys?" (he never touched her things). She didn't know her son had earned straight A's since eighth grade. It had occurred to him to tell her, but he always decided against it.

Johnny saw himself staying in Looking for the rest of his life. The thought simultaneously comforted and terrified him and anyways, leaving seemed impossible. Good grades didn't mean anything for him, or if they did, he didn't know what they meant, what they could be used for. He thought he could be a logger, or a mechanic, or a builder, maybe with his own business. His hands were calloused, there was old crud under all his nails (toes too) and he had dandruff.

He thought there was a difference between himself and someone like Hellie, who he knew would be able to do anything she put her mind to, whether or not she had the support of her father (which she would). She would be an artist or an English professor at one of those old universities with brick and ancient trees and people in clean clothes with no callouses. She would stay youthful forever and never get cavities and her skin would glow and not wrinkle because she would be away from the sea and the wind and the sun and the drugs that were so easy to get in Looking, from men and women in busted-up trailers and from the county clerk who spent a lot of time in the city. (Lennie could always tell the weeks when meth was circulating in town because people would come into the store with sunken eyes and clenching jaws and buy cigarettes and Coca-Colas for dinner even though they had kids at home, hungry.)

Johnny knew (hoped) that Hellie would be protected from

the elements and eat the best food and go to fancy bars and only drink one cocktail on Saturday nights with a boyfriend or a fiancé who loved her, a man who also grew up loved and so knew how to love. She would be treated well. She would not have her butt grabbed or be told to smile pretty or be cornered by mean and bored young men who liked to make women afraid for fun.

Imagining this future life for Hellie with this future man who loved her very much hurt his stomach. That's how he knew what he felt for her was love. Platonic love—a term he learned from something he saw online, which he also thought was the purest love. "Platonic," he sometimes said to himself under his breath, because he liked the sound of it against his teeth.

Johnny was sure he loved her because he had learned that love was very, very painful, at least for people like him: his mother told him she loved him all the time. "Dipshit," his mom would yell, and he would automatically respond, hating himself even more. He could see that he was being trained to be low like her. He could feel the tender place under his ribs getting smaller and smaller, shrinking. He knew it would disappear and he was afraid of what happened then, but he also knew what happened. He knew because he had uncles and none of them had any tender parts left.

On the internet, he read about an experiment where scientists exposed rats to a little bit of wind and a lot of wind and some rats got to be in a place with no wind. Turned out that the rats subjected to the most wind ended up chewing off their own limbs, starting with their hind legs. He hated knowing this but thought about it often. There was one winter when he was eight that he found a baby rat shivering and alone. He made a warm nest for it in the garage and gave it water and food scraps in secret. It sat on his arm and let him pet it and looked at him with intelligent eyes. When he was with the rat he didn't feel lonely. Any one of his friends would have killed the rat with a shovel or a hammer or a gun (Jason) or by throwing it in a bucket of water (Mike) or poisoning it or suffocating it (Greg) maybe stabbing it (Reggie) or putting it in a bag and running it over (Jake). He wasn't like them, but he was exactly like them because they were his people.

He took care of the rat for many months and then it was gone. At first he thought it would come back. Then he thought maybe his mom had found their hiding space and done something crazy, but nothing was out of place and she didn't yell at him that night. He settled on the idea that the rat hadn't loved him as much as he thought, that he hadn't worked hard enough to understand what the rat was trying to tell him with its eyes—the rat had given up on him and left. Or maybe the rat thought Johnny didn't love him enough and the rat's feelings were hurt. Johnny hated this more. He would rather be the one who carried the hurt than the one who caused the hurt. He thought what he could offer, and offer well, was to hold pain for others, that that was why he was here. The American flag tattoo was for his uncles, he realized, and wanted to find Hellie to tell her about this and the rat and that he loved her but not in the way of wanting to kiss her. The only person he wanted to kiss was Zeke, and Zeke had moved away last year to Idaho where he said all the men spend their time being psychotic and the women spend all their time pretending everything is fine.

Johnny had asked, "And what will you do there, in the mountains of Idaho?"

"I'll try hard to be more like the women," Zeke had said.

Lennie counted the cash drawer at Thompson's and thought

about how he didn't believe in forever anymore. He had been in love once, but now understood that everything died. Well, that sounded dramatic. He knew that change was inevitable. He used to look at Matthew's beautiful face and his heart would break each time. One of them would leave. One of them would fall out of love or find someone else to love or lose interest. One of them would want to have children and the other wouldn't want that at all. One of them would need a change or decide to move to Paris (alone). Or maybe one of them would have a motorcycle accident and die. Maybe cancer? Something. He knew that one of them could leave in the night without even a suitcase packed, no note.

A Buddhist he once met crossing the border from Canada into Washington told him that everything ends: it was the Dharma. She had stated it simply but firmly and he never forgot it. He used to talk with Matthew about growing old together, sitting on a bedraggled old couch somewhere and watching the seasons change. The thought was such a soothing balm, but he didn't let himself believe it. Not really. He would not be the kind of person to be lulled into such an unlikely fantasy. He knew that the majority of relationships ended in the first year, that more than half of marriages ended in divorce. He believed that this distance he maintained, this cynical perspective on romance is how he had been able to love so intensely because he never took love for granted. He was in it until he wasn't.

He couldn't focus on counting the change and looked out past the old pine tree that would surely blow over with the next wind gust and wondered for the first time: what if he had believed back then that his love could have lasted? And not as a couple who had been together forty years but only tolerated each other.

Lennie wondered if he and Matthew could have been

together, happy and connected, for their whole lives, actually end up on a porch swing somewhere watching hummingbirds and drinking hot tea and lamenting the first of their hairs turning gray and even later they could have called themselves two bald, old birdies and laughed about it—all in spite of what the Buddhist said, in spite of what Matthew feared, and what he had seen all around him since we was a child.

Esther understood that she was unlikable but didn't completely understand why. In her thirties (still just a child—that's how she described anyone pre-menopausal), she had made a list of things to remember when she was undeniably and officially "old."

Listen attentively, pay attention to people when they talk.
Don't complain about my hips, molars or bunions.
Start dressing nicer with brighter clothes and "fun" eyeglasses, everything impeccably fitted and tucked (to compensate for sagging skin).
Try harder to not care about sagging skin, sagging tits and sagging ass, but also...
Remember that if I let my face relax too much, I look very angry and disturbed.
Talk less, in general.
Don't laugh at my own jokes. Or do?
Be inquisitive, even when tired, irritated and fed up.
Leave anonymous presents for people: a trinket or a cupcake or a dollar bill.
Don't be such a Francophile and read more of the German philosophers.

Daniel pet his long beard as if comforting an old, wiry terrier, and asked Hellie how she was doing with the wind. She replied that she was enjoying it, but hadn't said anything because everyone else seemed so discombobulated. She said it's like a shower, like being scrubbed clean in a way that made her feel lighter, better. When he told her what he heard at the bar about a toddler blowing down the road she said, "Well, he won't even remember that when he's older. Isn't that strange? So much happens to us that we don't remember. That little kid can't hold the story, but we will until he's old enough."

Daniel wondered how she knew these things and liked that she had a philosopher's mind, that she thought about things and found pleasure in the thinking. He used to be that way too, but felt that Hellie's open inquisitiveness came directly from Sonya. He wondered if Sonya had seen that part of him early on when they first started dating—two teenagers who thought going to the movies one town over was the most exciting thing possible, that it made them grownups.

He used to like to ponder things more, would take his time on ideas and emotions too, turning them over like a stone in his pocket for days and weeks before he spoke them. He was a young adult who wanted to be sure of things. He wondered when that part of himself went quiet, when he became a man who thought his most important contribution was to make money to support his wife, then his daughter, which he had done without complaint. He knew that working was survival, but when had he stopped feeling things easily? Was he five? Was he eleven? He knew it happened early. He wanted to go back to his little-boy-self and say something. But what? Maybe that it was okay to have deep feelings besides anger, that it was okay to sit in the forest and think, daydream even, to lay on his back and watch the trees talk to each other. He felt a painful urge to go to the forest right then, but it was dark and how would he explain it to Hellie. To himself?

"Did you know Esther had the opportunity to study philosophy on a scholarship at the International School of Thought in Paris?" Daniel asked Hellie and she said yes, that once when she was nine Esther had pulled her aside and said, "You've got a wonderful mind, child. I can see it and others will see it too." And then Esther had given Hellie a strange, little shove that had almost knocked her over. "But you must be strong. Stronger than me. You have to stand up to the bastards," she had said, making her hands into two tight fists and shaking them at either Hellie or the sky—Hellie couldn't tell which—and then Esther had walked away without looking back.

Daniel continued, "She passed up the scholarship but never told anyone why. She and I used to talk about Foucault's ideas, about normalcy and othering. I'm not sure when we stopped talking like that, or why."

The thought of this hung in the air, both of them quiet, looking out at the field before them, tall grasses being blown sideways by big gusts, the trees' hair and arms flying everywhere all at once.

Tuesday, mid-morning Johnny's father called from a phone with no callback number and left a message. "Let go or be dragged, my boy. None of the world's heartbreak is your fault. Just let go. Just let go." Johnny played the message over and over, a hundred times, a thousand. He didn't know what his dad meant exactly, but he couldn't stop crying.

Hellie found the Ouija Board at the senior center thrift store, which is kind of the town living room where just about everything costs a dollar or less if you ask nicely. If you were rude to Mrs. Owens, who ran the place, prices were sure to go up.

Hellie had the board under her arm in a soft paper bag when she saw Johnny across the street on Esther's porch. She had imagined doing the Ouija alone when her dad was out, but something made her feet move towards Esther's house as the door opened a crack for Johnny, then a crack wider, for her.

The three of them found themselves at a dusty table with crumbly cookies and an old Sinatra record on the player skipping every third line.

"This fucking goddamn wind!" Esther said as her bird feeder blew off its hook outside the window. "What does it want?!"

It seemed both strange and perfectly normal that the three of them would find themselves here, not saying much as Hellie removed the board from its box.

Hellie read the instructions, faded to a light yellow, out loud:

One: Gather two or more people willing to communicate with the dead who are serious about it.

Two: Lower the lights and place candles nearby. Remove distractions, if possible.

Three: Invite the spirit to enter the space. Tell them it is safe and that you will listen to what they have to say.

Four: Start with easy "Yes" or "No" questions first. If the spirit is weak, you will get more information from them in this way.

Five: When the conversation is complete, remember to say "GOODBYE." This is a critical step to end the séance as you do not want any part of the spirit to linger.

All three were somber when Hellie finished reading. Esther glanced out the window and took a deep breath. Somehow they had begun, together, to realize the same thing.

"I know who we need to talk to," Esther said and looked down at her hands. "Johnny, you know you can't tell your family about this, right? They're not going to understand."

Johnny nodded, but looked like he might get up from the table and run. He took a deep breath and without thinking, reached out to hold both their hands as if he had done this before.

Hellie couldn't seem to say anything, knew what was about to happen somehow, and stared at the lit candle flickering in the draft from outside. Esther spoke first.

"Sonya, has it been you? I think it has, dear. I know it has. What would you like us to understand?"

The wind lulled, then picked up again. The board said nothing.

"Mama?" Hellie asked, sounding and feeling more like a little girl than she had in a long time.

"*Is* it you?" Still nothing.

Johnny felt afraid, but wanted this to work now, more than anything.

"Sonya? You've been blowing us around a little, huh? That's okay with me, Sonya. I think you're helping us somehow. What do you want us to understand?" he asked her. Hellie realized she'd never heard him string so many words together at one time.

But the board didn't do anything. The three of them sat in

the darkness of the room holding hands. It was too dark for them now to see if the wind was still blowing the trees or not. There was no sound at all except for their quiet breathing.

It was helpful in some ways to focus on the children we had left behind and we did so. We concentrated with everything we had, otherwise we knew our messages wouldn't go through to the living. We wanted to be helpful, mostly. We were genderless now, just specks of light, but we still had some influence, some strength. We missed our bodies that hadn't held up as portals, knew it wasn't the fault of the beings coming through, it was just what happened sometimes. We could feel ourselves leaving and there was nothing to do about it but say yes. Some of us said our goodbyes to our bodies in hospitals, wiped with disinfectant. Some in our living rooms, sitting in a warm tub of water. Some of us tried to stay quiet and some of us put a lot of effort into screaming—we wanted to go out with a bang. I still felt like myself, like the Sonya that existed, but I was part of something else now, something not singular.

None of us knew what was coming at first. We had taken birthing classes or read books or talked about it quietly with our mothers and grandmothers. Some of us watched YouTube alone in our apartments eating cereal, wrapped in tattered bathrobes. Most of us were at least a little bit scared. Most of us wanted to have the baby but a few of us didn't. Some of us had partners who would say encouraging things and rub our feet and bring the ice cream, broccoli, or peanut butter we desired, and some of us were alone or wished we were.

We knew how to move through time and we knew how to haunt.

We knew how to visit the living through dreams and wind and snow and rain, and we knew when to do nothing. Sometimes one of us would say to another, "I can't believe you did that!" like we were still alive and talking on the phone, no big deal. Another of us would say, "You only live once," and we would all nod our heads, suddenly serious.

We all visit our children regularly. We attempt to add a little levity. We try to help them sleep better. We rub their heavy shoulders when they're upset and sometimes we put a little piece of candy under the couch cushion for them to find. We know how to delight. We still know how to cry but don't need to. We know what was lost and tears don't help anymore.

We could not have known that, even here, from this vast distance, things could change so quickly. We looked out into space and wished we still had tense foreheads to rub—we missed the feel of our aging skin. We could not have known how hard it would be to watch our babies' bodies morph into new, older beings that we were even less familiar with. To see our old lovers age and wrinkle and ache. We could not have known that in the face of a real problem, a real catastrophe, we could not help our children as much as we would have liked to think—they were so far away. We didn't understand at first, these ancient constraints, but we were starting to. These things take time.

The wind was my idea and the others helped. We wanted them to have something to rail against together. We noticed how lonely everyone was, going about their own business, lost in their own heads and fears and daydreams. We were uncertain if our strategy was working or not and were getting tired of blowing without proof that our goals were being achieved.

"Guess it doesn't work," Johnny said. "Unless you guys felt something?"

Esther had her eyes closed, and was kind of rocking back and forth. Hellie stared at the wooden pointer, begging it to start moving on its own but it was still. They were holding hands and none of them wanted to let go. Finally Johnny stood abruptly and apologized, saying he should be getting home.

When the door closed behind him, Esther's voice came out raspy. "Do you know about Jean-Paul Sartre?" Esther asked Hellie in the darkness. Neither of them moved. "He once said, 'Life begins on the other side of despair.'"

"Isn't that beautiful?" Esther asked, and Hellie nodded, not knowing if her despair had already happened or would happen in the future. *Probably both*, she thought, feeling very grown up.

"Your life has begun," Esther said, reading her mind. "And you are so alive. You're a whole person and you are incredibly alive."

Daniel found a bone on the rare morning he permitted himself to not be productive and instead went for a walk on the dark, gray beach. He knew immediately it was human, having set so many bones in his life for so many stupid men.

"It's an ulna bone, probably male, right arm," he said when he handed it to Marcos. When Marcos didn't seem very surprised, Daniel knew this wasn't the first human bone that'd been found recently.

"Let me know if I can do anything to help, Sheriff," Daniel

said as he left, a set of teeth starting to gnash in his gut.

As he pushed open the front door, he looked back, fighting the urge to run back and grab the bone and take it with him. He wanted to construct a whole skeleton, let Hellie give the body a name, set it up in the hallway where it would always be there waiting to welcome them home.

Lennie sat alone at the register. Everything was done, but he didn't want to go home. The store lights were off, except for the flashing neon that stayed on in the front. There was a faint metallic smell from the side of beef the butcher had been making his cuts from all afternoon.

Lennie could not stop ruminating on the plans he and Matthew had made all those years ago. They had been passing through Looking on motorcycles, on a trip from Canada that would take them all the way to the southernmost tip of Argentina—Tierra del Fuego. They had saved money and schemed—decided they could be away for a year. Lennie thought their plan was bulletproof when it was actually punctured with holes. The first hole: engine problems, the second and fatal hole, something far worse: he loved Matthew, but he was miserable. He did not want to go on.

Matthew had given up everything for their trip. He had left his other lovers behind, pawned everything he owned, kissed his lonely mother goodbye, and believed in Lennie and the plan they had hatched. He was ready to be transformed. "The trip of a lifetime," he had kept saying. But Lennie had backed out, said he couldn't, didn't want to, changed his mind. Lennie thought he should be happy with Matthew, who was sexy and fun and beautiful and kind, who everyone loved to be around, but he wasn't happy and he could not get out from under the weight of that feeling. He knew a long trip would have made it worse—made him feel lonely and dishonest and lowly and ashamed.

I'm unhappy, Matthew. I'm not myself. It's not your fault, but this isn't right for me anymore. I'm so sorry. He had been up all night trying to write a letter to Matthew that would mean something, over and over until his hand felt like it was going to break, trying to make something make sense. He wanted the tenderness he felt to be visible on a piece of paper, out of his body and tangible in some way. In the morning, bleary-eyed and strung out, anxious bile thick in his intestines, he had texted his words instead and immediately regretted it. He hadn't been brave enough to look Matthew in the eye—to hand him a piece of real paper, let alone sit down and say it. He had panicked. He was a coward, but it wasn't for a lack of effort. He thought he was doing a favor to Matthew by backing out when he did, not wanting to waste any more of anyone's time.

He wasn't sure he knew how to love anyone well. He wasn't sure what all this was for, this messy life. When diagnosed with early-stage cancer his friend Oliver had made the decision to go without any medical intervention, that he was okay to leave if that's what the cards had dealt him. He tidied up his life, had a going-away party where he explained to his close friends the trip he was about to make to Switzerland where assisted suicide—for any of the reasons someone might want to die—was legal. He could have stayed in Oregon to do it but he wanted "one last trip." What he hadn't told them is he wanted to do it alone. He said he would be in a warm room, beige he imagined, with his favorite song playing—Radiohead's "How to Disappear Completely."

"Not a subtle song choice," Lennie had said, trying to find humor in the misery.

"I know! Fuck. I'm so emo," Oliver had said and laughed. They had all laughed—their last laugh together. Their last cry too.

Lennie missed Oliver but knowing there was a safe place, should he also decide to leave for good, comforted him immensely. *You punched me in the face and you're telling me your hand hurts*, he heard Matthew moan over and over in his mind when he was alone in the dark at three in the morning with the rain coming down and a tree frog croaking out a song to the forlorn trees. He looked at the two ravens out his window with their huge beaks and sleek heads and knew, even though he got so depressed and anxious sometimes, that he made the right decision.

He looked closer at the bird on the left. *Was that a bone in her beak? Wait. Was that a finger?*

Marcos didn't really know what to do with three human bones and no leads, no missing persons, and no one responding to his calls from the county. He wished he could bury them in the vast forest behind Thompson's, erase their existence from the collective memories of Johnny, Daniel, and Lennie and just go back to doing his daily Sudoku.

The wind had been too much for everyone and the announcement of these bones would push some right over the edge. When he went outside to smoke a cigarette on his porch, something felt wrong. He looked at the opaque sky, the still trees, the birds splashing in the mud puddle in the driveway and sighed. It wasn't windy. It hit him like its own kind of gust.

"You've left us?" he asked out loud, slapping his palm against his thigh and wanting to laugh. He felt indescribable relief. He felt so grateful for the stillness.

The problem of the bones didn't seem like such a terrible burden anymore. Up the old road, badly potholed and in need of repairs, Esther came out and looked up at the tree leaves, letting it sink in, this new stillness. Hellie sat at her desk and started drawing up plans for her School of Death which would be built right there in Looking, where people from all over the world who were or were not afraid of death would come to study. Johnny searched online for Simone de Beauvoir and found a translation of her book *The Ethics of Ambiguity*. He texted Zeke, *I miss you*, but didn't feel lonely and realized with some comfort that he didn't need a response. Daniel picked up some gummy bears and a small bouquet of carnations at the store for Hellie as a surprise. Lennie opened an old philosophy textbook and found a quote by Sartre. He read it over and over and even though he couldn't quite be sure he knew what it meant, he felt compelled to write it in cursive across his entire forearm in black permanent marker, slowly scrawling:

Like all dreamers, I mistook disenchantment for truth.

And beyond them, throughout Looking, others were noticing the change in the wind too, and everyone, including the ravens, took a deep breath

in and out,

in and out, in and out.

Gymnogyps

Our son Jesse is fourteen and no longer willing to leave the house. Clea and I have both tried talking to him about it, but he just replies with grunts and door slams. After various failed attempts, I resort to my most desperate and unskilled strategy, the one that drives Clea insane, but usually works.

"Jesse, ten bucks if you just tell me why you won't go outside anymore."

He eyes me coolly. He's got these gray eyes that are unnerving even when he's in a good mood, which is almost never these days.

"I don't need your money, Elke," he tells me. Lately he's been calling me by my first name. (My therapist assures me this is normal and to not dwell on it too much.) Then Jesse pauses like he pities me and explains, "The graphics on my computer are way better than *out there*."

He says *out there* like he's getting a terrible taste out of his mouth, trying to spit it hard, like the loogies he used to launch off our front porch at innocent pedestrians. We were mortified when we found out and forced him to go house to house to apologize to all our victimized neighbors.

"He's just rebelling against you two with this not-going-outside phase," my therapist tells me. She peers out at me from her flowy therapy garb like a little hedgehog. "Don't you and Clea do a lot in the great outdoors?" she asks.

It's true; Clea and I both love being in nature. In the summers when Jesse is out of school and can stay with Clea's parents in Spokane, we go backpacking as much as we can. Clea and I have been joking for years about how we're becoming our elderly mothers by getting really into birdwatching.

"This is the most boring hobby imaginable," Jesse said several summers ago, before the not-going-outside phase, when he was only eleven and we took him down to the redwoods across the Oregon border into California. I told him about the California Condor and its scientific name, *Gymnogyps californianus*, to get him more interested. Every once in a while Jesse can get excited about something like a scientific name. He likes that kind of knowing, of classifying. I told him the Yurok tribe was rehabilitating them and releasing them into the wild—that we had to drive to California to try to see one but that by the time he was my age maybe they'd be flying over Oregon too, as they once did over a century ago. I took a tentative breath, imagining Jesse in his late forties.

"Condors have almost a ten-foot wingspan and are basically a direct descendant of the dinosaurs," I told him, knowing it would take an unlikely miracle for one of these giant birds to appear. I was just pleased that for a moment he was listening with genuine curiosity.

We packed a picnic with all his favorite foods, one of the sugary drinks he begs for that we almost never let him have, and the promise of extra video game time that night if he didn't ruin things for everyone.

But he did ruin things; he always ruins things.

He asked to go to the car and we figured he just wanted to get out of the sun, sit on something soft for a bit. But when I went to check on him, I found he had taken a shit on the ground by the muffler, picked most of it up, and wiped it all over the back windshield of our car. While Clea and I were looking out over the cool waters at all the great blue herons, Jesse was rinsing the rest of the shit off his hands with what was left of his picnic drink.

"At least he had the consideration to wipe his poop on the *outside* of the window," Clea said.

She's always looking on the bright side.

I went into my therapist's office that week unsuccessfully fighting back tears. I've told her so many stories like this over the years, but it's hard to know what to do about Jesse. When he was younger, we got him the full barrage of tests—psychological, emotional, nutritional, physical, neurological. Was it gut health? Schizophrenia? We had him tested for learning differences, for autism spectrum, and for allergies. We even talked to a psychic. All this, and no answer presented itself. He doesn't fit into any easy boxes and refuses to go to therapy.

Clea says, "I don't want him to feel like there's something wrong with him. It's called being an 'identified patient.' At this age if he's not willing, it could really affect his identity and self-esteem."

More and more often when she says things like this, I imagine tying a thick rope around my neck and the satisfying sound of breaking vertebrae if I were to step off the tall stool in the basement.

"Maybe forcing him to get help with whatever he's got going on now will help him not be a full-blown sociopath later on?" I ask, my voice lilting up into a question even though I don't want it to.

"Please don't pathologize our son," Clea says. "He's just a bit challenging, and besides, that's not how sociopathy works."

My therapist tries to stay neutral but seems to agree with Clea. It's possible I just have a terrible therapist. It feels like I'm in some gaslighter's funhouse and everyone is in on it but me, because when I see Jesse, hear him, and smell him, I know in my gut there's something very wrong. But then again, maybe there's just something wrong with me. I think I'm normal, but maybe everyone thinks they're normal.

When Jesse was younger, I put in so much care and effort. I was the one who stayed at home with Jesse when Clea went back to work after his birth. I've been there, fully present and trying, for the teething, the tantrums, the bed-wetting, the refusing to go to school, the violent outbursts, the door kicking, the punching, the rage, the nascent misogyny, the sadistic humor, the computer addiction, and the atrocious hygiene. It's been so much work and lately it doesn't feel worth it. I don't understand how I've arrived at this place where nothing I've done seems to have mattered to anyone, least of all me. I know many teenagers are self-absorbed and difficult, but to say Jesse takes it to a new level is a grotesque understatement. He is disturbed and disturbing and I can't stop thinking that it is all my fault.

I've never said this to anyone, not even my therapist, because it's such heteronormative thinking, but I wonder if all the unease I feel is because I'm not the one who birthed him—that we didn't create the right kind of bond. Before deciding to have a baby, everyone we talked with about gay families who use a sperm donor said it wouldn't really matter in the grand scheme of things—we would both be his parents, and together we would form a cohesive family. I've always known I didn't want to ever physically birth a child—even before I fully understood my androgynous gender, the thought of childbirth appalled me. None of this probably even matters. All I know for sure is that I've been trying really hard for so long and now I'm very tired.

"Sometimes it happens that even when family members love each other, they really don't like each other," my therapist says this week. "That can be hard to accept, and makes it harder to conveniently place blame, harder to know what to do."

As we're winding down the session she adds, "Suffering is just what happens when we don't accept the truth of what is."

I think about this all week. Maybe the truth is that I don't like my son and my fighting against it is what's causing all this pain. These days I find myself frequently lost in daydreams where I never again have to see any of the people I love. It's like Clea and Jesse are just going along, and I'm living in some alternate reality where I'm the only one who still balks when Jesse screams to Clea that she's a "dumb cunt," whereby she calmly responds, "I don't want to be talked to like that," and he finishes up by saying he doesn't give a fuck what she wants, but within fifteen minutes they're on the couch together laughing about some asinine YouTube video like nothing even happened. I'm afraid to find out what the effect of days and months and years of this behavior is, but a sense that I already know is what keeps me wide awake and staring at the ceiling most nights.

Sometimes the only way I can calm down is thinking about Camus. I read *The Myth of Sisyphus* in high school and remember that opening line about how the only serious philosophical problem is that of suicide, and that answering whether or not one finds life worth living is the most basic of questions. It comforts me, thinking of Camus. That alone could be cause for alarm, but sometimes I imagine Camus is sitting next to me, in the car, or on a bench at the park while I'm wading through all these dark thoughts. It makes me feel so much better to think of him in this genial way, like he's just a quiet person who works in my office and sometimes we go out for a cocktail and have a meaningful conversation.

Whether or not I can conjure up Camus, this thinking that I don't want to be here anymore is taking up more and more of my thoughts. In line at the grocery store, I get Jesse the canned chili he loves to dump over a pile of beige hot dogs lying on his plate like cadaverous penises. When he eats, he wipes his hands all over the front of his shirt like a toddler and doesn't notice he has huge chunks of beans and meat stuck to his face and neck. What I think about next, as I'm checking out, is how many pills it would take to knock myself out eternally, and where I could get them.

When I type in *how to kill myself* on the internet, there aren't even any websites with good ideas—all the top postings are for suicide hotlines and where to get help. This feels like a real 21st century betrayal. I reach out to my nurse friend Nadine, who told me that barbiturates are out of fashion these days: better to get ahold of some insulin and opiates.

"It's much harder than it seems to kill oneself," she told me. "Just last week an ICU nurse tried to kill herself with Ativan plus some Ambien and something else. She came through just fine. Me? To really get the job done? I'd just use a sharp knife to slit my jugular."

Nurses are so hard to fluster.

I don't think Nadine suspected anything strange from my

line of questioning—just casual conversation to a nurse.

Sometimes I think about suicide in the car too, driving up these winding Oregon coastal roads with sheer cliffs below. It would be all too easy to just swerve off and plummet over the edge. I wonder how many people go through with it, probably many, and then I wonder how long it takes for their cars and bodies to be found. Then I keep going and arrive in the driveway without a scratch, but make a mental note to look up those statistics later.

My father used to try to kill himself. Sometimes when my mom and I went out we would come home and find him half inside of the oven, with the pilot light out and the gas cranked up high. It was unsettling but even at that young age I somehow knew that he wasn't really trying too hard, what with the open backdoor letting all that fresh air in. He just seemed so defeated, with his bony knees on the stained linoleum and his upper body resting on the pot roast rack. After this happened several times, I sealed myself off from the grayness surrounding him as much as I could. I still tried to be a good child, to make them proud. I went to Mass with them once a year when my father's car needed to pass a smog test, or when he was hoping for a promotion; we were those kinds of Catholics. We really didn't talk about anything, me and my parents, which is why I keep trying to get Jesse to open up to me, even though it's getting expensive. I want something different for him.

The thing is, nothing has happened to Jesse. At least I'm pretty sure. No one has molested him, there have been no violent backhands—not even a light spank. Sometimes I wonder if he was traumatized in a past life since nothing else makes sense. Clea insists he's just a sensitive boy growing up in our fascist, capitalistic American society, and gives me a look that makes me feel like I'm not only crazy, but cruel, and maybe even stupid.

Tonight after dinner, I sit with my laptop and search the Aokigahara Forest in Japan where so many people go to end their lives. Looking at pictures, the forest seems alluring, and at the same time knowing how much death it contains is overwhelming—but not necessarily in a bad way. All that lush green, those twisted roots, all those bones. It's kind of beautiful, really, a place like that.

Not far from that redwood forest we haven't been back to since the incident with Jesse's feces, there's a wilderness area called Big Springs with enough acreage to really get lost. There are black bears there—also mountain lions, bobcats, rattlesnakes, and vultures. I read recently that they are reintroducing more California Condors in Big Springs too. I guess it wasn't so far-fetched that we could have seen one with Jesse that day. I wish we had. Maybe it would have made all the difference somehow.

Learning more about Aokigahara gives me the idea that maybe I could die in Big Springs. I could hike in, take off all my clothes in a kind of ancestral ritual—a letting go of identity, of what was. Then I could make my way through the forest naked to a very hard-to-get-to secret spot, dig most of a hole and bury myself alive before finally shooting myself full of insulin. If I could find the right spot it's possible no one would ever find me. Or I could scramble my way up some rocky precipice, lay my body out to the open sky, channel Nadine, and slit my own throat, then wait for some scavenger to smell the blood and land beside me. I imagine a young Gymnogyps landing on my stiff, cold chest and taking that first strong peck.

I fall into a deep sleep feeling serene, like I can smell the dirt, rocks, pine trees, and musty feathers already.

Jesse wakes me up, which is very unusual and I see it is mid-morning. It startles me to see Jesse there, standing next to the bed, like he did when he was little and wanted blueberry pancakes for breakfast.

"What's happened? Is everything okay?" I ask, sitting up as I try to shake the sleep from my head.

"Are you going to do it?" he asks me.

"Do what?" I ask, really confused, like maybe I've forgotten I promised to take him somewhere—like he is still a person who goes outside and does things.

"I looked at your search history," he says, with those gray eyes cutting right through me. "You've been so weird when you're on your laptop lately. I thought you were watching porn."

"I haven't been watching porn," I say, still trying to clear my head.

"Yeah, but I was right that something was off. So, are you going to do it or not?" he asks.

With a jolt I realize he's found my Aokigahara forest image searches, Highway 101 death statistics, lists of suicide hotline numbers I didn't even want, and my online copy of *The Myth of Sisyphus*.

"I've just been thinking about forests and birds a lot, philosophical stuff," I say, confusing even myself.

"I'll start going outside again," Jesse says, "Sorry I mess everything up."

My heart starts pounding then and there's a ringing in my ears. I feel like I might throw up and all I want is to take everything back, start over from the very beginning, and somehow try harder to make it alright for him, for myself too. For all of us.

But I don't know how.

We stay still and quiet right where we are, with the morning sun coming through the window, and a condor somewhere, not too far south, flying slow, heavy circles over the tallest trees.

Willamette

Dusk on the river was darkly bruised, exhausted. The putrid spew from the mushroom canning factory up the road sputtered into nothingness as evening fell, and even the semi-trucks that passed on their way from the fields to I-5 rumbled slowly like they were tired. Mom was in the kitchen steaming artichokes and smoking Lucky Strikes out the window.

"Babe, look, the sky's the exact color of a blood orange."

We both stood there looking out at the deep-red ending of the day, thinking our own thoughts. Though there was yelling in our house sometimes, we could also be very quiet together. She cut gloves at the leather warehouse along the Willamette River. Eight hours of heavy, metal scissors following the outlines of five fingers, gloves others would wear for protection while her own hands became raw and stiff in the making of them. She was twenty-nine and I was nine, and she told me those twenty years between us were our lucky number. When playing the lottery, as we did once a year, a twenty always made it into our numerical selections.

"That was the number of years here on earth without you," she'd say, and though I knew she loved me, what I heard in her voice was an underlying sentiment of loss.

Clyde Crawford had warm skin like he had just been taken

from the oven and his face was round and smooth. It was easy to imagine exactly what he had looked like as a boy. But even with his youthful face, he had a pillowy gut from cases of beer and his breath smelled of yeast. He tended to the vast fields of hops plants in late spring and summer, until harvest started in August. Strawberries in the early part of the summer and apples and pears toward the end. He was from a small town in Ohio and he told stories of his family there, his time as a kid growing up. He hadn't gone to school past fifth grade.

"No one there had nothing. Nothing at all," he told us. "And my mother," he said, with a mix of what seemed to be both pride and shame, "was so tall that people often thought she was a transvestite."

We nodded, wondering where this was going.

"But no," he said after a long silence in which it seemed he had started thinking about something else. "She just had a strong jawline. And she for sure had a pussy."

Then he laughed a low, rumbly laugh and looked to see if he'd gone too far, if he had succeeded in shocking us. He didn't know us well enough to understand it was more difficult than one might think. We had seen things.

Once at a gas station when I was around seven, we were waiting for our turn at the pump in the battered, blue Volkswagen Beetle Mom drove, the metal so eroded we could see the road pass by underneath us through the floorboards. The gas station attendant was young with tan skin, acne, and smiling eyes. As he started walking over to our car, he burst into flames. The gas pump nearest him did too. Mom started to scream and tried to cover my eyes. Then she got out to see if she could help, but other people were there by then. She returned to the car out of breath and we drove away, over the curb and out of there.

"Was he smoking a cigarette or something?" I asked. I had seen something like this on TV once.

She nodded inconclusively, reached for a cigarette to calm her nerves, then thought better of it and shoved it into the ashtray. We never went back to that gas station again and on the occasions we passed by it on our way to someplace else, all I could think of was that burning boy coming towards us with his kind eyes.

For this, and other reasons that had to do with Mom's previous boyfriends and living in Felony Flats—the nickname for the neighborhood directly surrounding the Oregon State Penitentiary—when Clyde told us about his tall, manly mother and her pussy, we just listened, taking it in. He circled back to this story more than once, like he was stuck in it or wanted us to figure something out about him, about where he came from. Sometimes it seemed Mom didn't quite know what to make of Clyde, but she never seemed surprised.

"I once dated someone who lied about having served in Vietnam," Mom said. "I think he wanted an excuse for all his fucked-up behavior. Why else would someone lie about that? Did he think there was any honor in it, killing innocent brown people for America? I just wish he hadn't punched in all the walls in the bedroom. Remember that, Babe?"

I did remember, and I got a secret thrill when she included me in her adult conversations. She drifted off and Clyde kept going. Clyde's mother's name was Veronica. His father, Jack, was a relatively unknown entity who his mother said was rough and beautiful and had traveled the country hopping trains and hitchhiking. Apparently, he was a singer, "a good lovemaker," and not the type to stay in one place, with one person.

"You got his looks," Clyde's mother had told him, "but I hope you're not the type to run away from the people who need you."

Clyde told us he didn't know what type of person he was and looked sheepishly at Mom. She didn't seem too concerned with Clyde being the type of person to run away or not. She didn't seem needy with Clyde like I'd seen her before with other men. What Clyde brought out in her was a new, loose kind of calm. Her shoulders softened and she laughed more. Sometimes she would play her guitar for us and I held on to those moments the most. Inevitably, a tangible shift would waft in, and it was my bedtime. Usually, soon after, I could hear their animal noises through the thin walls of our worn down duplex.

A lot of people said when they first met me they couldn't tell if I was a boy or a girl and I liked that. Though Mom never called me anything other than Babe, she had officially named me Smokey because that "Cruisin" song was on the radio constantly when she was pregnant. Unlike many women about to have a baby, she didn't have cravings for food, but she did have cravings for those verses.

"The feeling I got listening to it was like..." she drifted off, remembering.

"Just listen for yourself," she said, back when she first put the song on the record player for me. I could see what she meant and I think I loved the song as much as she had that summer. Even though I didn't fully understand it, it became my anthem.

When I got older, kids on the playground teased me about my name.

"Your mom must really like to smoke," they'd snicker.

That was true, but I knew the secret: I was named after a smooth, soulful singer with perfect cheekbones and straight, gleaming teeth, not like all the Salem snaggletooths who filled Auburn Elementary School. It was years later Mom told me she used to date Smokey Robinson's cousin up in Portland.

"They look exactly alike," she said. "So when the guy told me he was related to Smokey on his dad's side, I completely believed him." I imagined her still dating him, us both getting to see those Robinson family green eyes every day. But we didn't have Smokey's cousin, instead we had Clyde.

When there were no crops to pick, Clyde liked to drink beer. Sometimes he helped out around our house, fixing a fence or repairing a leaky faucet, but mostly he drank. Some afternoons I'd come home from school and he'd be there while Mom was still at work. We didn't have much to say to each other, I realized. Mom was the bridge between us, and without her, we were just two people who found ourselves sharing a small space. Once I asked him where he lived when he wasn't staying with us.

"With five assholes in a trailer off Highway 99 in Gervais," he said.

So it made sense to me that Clyde was spending more time at our house. His red truck could often be found in our driveway, like a beacon or a warning. From his rearview mirror hung an air freshener depicting Jude the Apostle in faded technicolor. Sometimes when I came home from school he was asleep, other times fidgety, like he'd done something wrong, but when I looked around, everything seemed normal. Even so, when he was there in those hours before Mom got home from work, I would often go to a friend's house, stay at the school library, or play games in the large, dusty field behind the mushroom cannery with all the other kids who didn't want to go home.

About six months into Mom dating Clyde, the first signs appeared. I came home earlier than usual and Clyde was passed out on the couch with the TV on. I looked over on the way to my room: in his hand was his dick, huge and limp. I could not take my eyes off its size and shape. I had seen Mom's *Joy of Sex* book and thumbed through *Our Bodies, Ourselves*, but this was different. The air had a musky smell and Clyde seemed serene. I had been around Clyde when he was sleeping before and knew him to be a deep sleeper, so I was caught off guard when Clyde opened his eyes to catch me staring at him. I expected him to be embarrassed by his dick hanging out, but he wasn't. He looked at me with sleepy eyes and slowly ran his hand over it once, finally pushing it down into his stretched-out underwear, slowly zipping up his jeans. Then, he closed his eyes with a strange calm. I said nothing and walked quickly to my room and shut the door, but I could hear him chuckling quietly to himself as, outside my window, our backyard gate clanked shut. I peeked out to see Jeremiah, our twenty-year-old neighbor looking at our house, catching my eye. I smiled and waved at him like always.

Later that night, Mom sensed my tenseness and asked me three times if I was alright, but I had nothing to say. Clyde was doing the dishes and playfully slapping her on the ass with a dish towel and her concern faded. Later that night I could hear their animal sounds, only this time the difference was I had a clear, disconcerting image of what the involved body parts were. I imagined Clyde's calm face as Mom moaned through the walls.

Over ten-thousand years ago, the Kalapuya Indians named the river Whilamut, which means "where the river ripples and runs fast." The name was altered sometime in history and its current pronunciation is still a good way to tell if someone is a local or not. The Willamette is one of only a few rivers that flows to the north, instead of to the south, spanning 187 miles between the Oregon coast and the Columbia River. The Willamette itself is a sleepy snake, wide and muddy, deceptive. In winter it swells up, covering beaches and banks, flooding houses, rising up to the bottoms of bridges, swirling in dirty eddies, eating trees. In the summer months, its coolness lures people in. From the banks, the flow looks like a gentle meandering, but in reality it has one of the fiercest undertows of any river. On *Today in Oregon*, there is report after report of people entering the river and not resurfacing until days later when the current decides it has done enough and throws them back up at its indifferent leisure.

The spring of Clyde and his dick was unusually warm and dry and it felt like summer had come early for once. The first river accident of the season that year was Danny Tucker, who was four when his family went out in a raft after picnicking over in West Salem, across the bridge. The raft capsized quickly and all of them went under. Within seconds everyone resurfaced except Danny. June came and it seemed like all anyone talked about was the missing body of that boy. From pictures in the paper over the next few weeks, I found myself thinking that if he was somehow found alive and had a chance to grow up, he would have looked a lot like our neighbor Jeremiah, and in my mind, I created a connection between the two. At dinner that night, I showed Mom and Clyde the picture.

"Doesn't he look like a kid version of Jeremiah?" I asked them.

Clyde let a strange look move across his face and Mom said,

"Sure, kinda. I think I see what you mean," but she was distracted making vegetable soup.

My school had an emergency assembly to talk about water safety and the importance of always wearing a life jacket. Discounted swim classes were offered at the community center, altars could be found along the river's shores, and water safety warnings were broadcast on the news every night at five. Some older kids I knew rode their bikes along the river, hoping to be the ones to find Danny's body, but I didn't want anything to do with that. I was, however, fascinated with the idea, the reality of a body not resurfacing, and how it must feel underneath all that dirty wetness. I imagined the river as a heavy blanket you couldn't find a way out from, holding you down until you got too tired and fell asleep beneath it.

Jeremiah had never left home and lived a few houses down with his dad. He worked on cars in their driveway for cash, and Mom had hired him a few times for help with the Volkswagen, whose sputters had steadily increased. I still associated our car with the gas station and felt an unease about even short trips around town. I wanted a different car, but Mom said we had to keep the one we had running for as long as we could. Jeremiah still looked like a teenager with a cuteness about him that prevented me—or anyone else—from seeing him as a grown man. He was still a boy with no facial hair, usually wearing his fading varsity jacket.

It was Mom who found them together a couple months later. There was an electrical fire at the warehouse and they sent all the workers home early. I was still at school. She wasn't surprised to see Clyde's truck in the driveway, but she was surprised by what she saw inside. She just stood there looking through the living room window from the outside, suddenly and intensely, an outsider. Clyde was leaned back on the couch and Jeremiah was on his knees with his own pants unzipped, leaning towards Clyde's dick. She didn't tell me any of these details until years later, and when she finally did, I think she expected me to be more surprised than I was. I could imagine it so easily: football on the TV, sweat stains spreading. I'd never told her about what I'd seen for myself those months before—what eventually I put together without any help.

When I got home on that particular day I didn't know exactly what had happened. I just knew Clyde was out of our lives. His few things were gone and so was his truck. The only proof he had ever been there was a trail of oil that spotted the driveway. The house didn't smell like yeast or musk anymore. Mom was scrubbing the couch with steaming hot water and a strong detergent, her knuckles pink and angry.

"Danny Tucker's body resurfaced today," I said cautiously, watching her back as it moved with the effort of scrubbing. "They told us in school. They found him over by the Boise Mill."

She unbent herself, turned around, and looked at me carefully. I was surprised to see some tears: she rarely cried.

"We're going to get a new car," she told me. "Jeremiah's not going to be working on our old one anymore."

I flashed from Danny to Jeremiah to the car to the boy at the gas station, flames around his skinny shoulders.

"You know I love you Babe, right?"

I nodded.

"Will you put the song on for us?" she asked.

I knew the one she meant. I walked across the living room, past her bucket of hot water and soap and put the needle down on the record. My namesake's perfect voice filled the air, solid and clear. I turned the music up and it drifted over to settle on our young skin, slowly floating us to the surface, river water under bones.

A Home in Beaver Palace

Buster (Fall 2003)

It took me a moment to recognize him as I stepped onto the bus—his old, easy smile and birdlike features had morphed into something bloated and unwell. Damp from the rain, he smelled desperately sour, and I thought of the last time I threw up.

I knew his name was Lorenzo. He had been a friend of Neil, my older brother. I hadn't seen Lorenzo in about seven years, back when Neil died. There were a lot of people I hadn't seen since then. Everyone had come together briefly for the funeral, like a spark in the dark, then quickly dispersed into nothingness.

Neil's nickname for me had been Buster and I always felt a jolt of satisfaction when he called it out to me. It meant someone understood who I was on the inside—tough and capable and not to be messed with. Our parents did not approve of this name and continued to call me Beatrice. Sometimes, in a rare playful moment, Beaver. (I have two big teeth with a gap in the middle.)

When Neil died, they didn't stop to grieve. Instead they overwhelmed themselves with work and travel. It's hard to explain but they got colder somehow—their sadness had a temperature. They were always very hard on Neil, our father especially. He had a softness that Dad couldn't tolerate—it sent him into rages.

There were angry lectures that Neil tolerated, where he had to remain silent and make eye contact the whole time...or else the belt, up until and past the time that Neil was too old and too big for the belt. I knew that Neil took the brunt of it so I wouldn't have to. I was ten when Neil died, seventeen now. No one calls me Buster anymore.

Outside the bus windows, there were so many trees. This is a city of trees, I thought, not a city of roses. No. It's a city of sad boys. An Elliott Smith song played in the back of my mind.

Lorenzo was staring at me with that confused look of not quite being able to place someone. He must have been twenty-five, the same age Neil would have been, but he looked much older. His teeth were yellowed, his hair matted, and he wore an army jacket stained with sweat and other, darker things. His eyes were glassy as he stared.

"Aren't you Neil's little sister?" he asked, voice cracking. I was surprised he got it right.

When I nodded, he looked like he didn't know what to say next, probably thinking of our lost commonality, the sharp jab that Neil was no longer with us. Lorenzo looked down at his hands and quietly spoke. "I'm not doing too good."

He couldn't have known it, but that's what Neil had said to me too that morning, his last one.

"Buster, I'm not doing too good," Neil had said, before looking away.

I hadn't known what to say to Neil, but sometimes when he was sad, I could still make him laugh by telling a joke or doing something silly. My favorite thing was to be the monster in *Young Frankenstein*, wide eyes beaming at him in the kitchen, my stiffened body banging into the dishwasher. But he hadn't laughed that last time, and when he left the room he barely patted my shoulder, already a ghost.

"I love you, Buster," he'd said, walking towards his room.

I thought things were normal and I'd left to go to my friend Jackie's house. We got on her dad's old computer and scrolled through his search history—all porn—and giggled at the unreal, absurd tits we found there. At that same exact time, alone at home, Neil took a bottle of pills, drew a hot bath, and slit his wrists, not leaving a note. His layered actions let us know he had meant for it to work. Not a warning. A determination.

I looked up and Lorenzo was staring at me, wondering where I'd gone, or maybe lost in his own thoughts.

"I'm not doing well," he repeated like an apology.

In spite of his rankness I moved closer to him, thinking of Neil. I told him he wasn't alone, that there were people who could help him. I wondered if most boys wanted to die or if it was just the ones I knew. I couldn't tell if Lorenzo was listening to me or if he believed what I was saying about there being help out there—good, kind people who would listen. Outside the window of the bus, Douglas fir trees swayed in the wind. The sky was wet and heavy, like it had been for weeks.

I looked at our reflection in the dark window, hoping he trusted me enough to stay.

After that, I saw Lorenzo a few more times. We met at an old diner off Burnside a year later, talked about bands we liked and movies we wanted to see. We talked about parties and smoking weed and how the liquor store off 34th Street never carded when he and Neil were my age. We talked about Neil too, but less often. He was always there under the surface of everything. I knew I was in over my head with Lorenzo, that all I could do was show up and listen. I've learned that's all we really can do, just be there, and that people are going to do whatever it is that calls to them, no matter what we think is best, no matter what it is we want.

Neil (Summer 1996)

The trees were swaying and even with all the rain, the stench of urine pooled in the corner of the bus stop, chewed gum spit on the ground forming a constellation, and a cold wind blowing through it all. There was a storm coming in from the sea, blowing inland across the whipped cream waves to find me in a too-thin jacket, weaving through trees I've known my whole life. It was only the first night but I could already smell myself, a sourness around the armpits creeping up my neck. I walked faster to keep warm, did some jumping jacks at the road that leads to the dump, and headed to our secret spot.

"You made it," said Lorenzo, making his way out from behind some trees, across the wet grass. "I didn't know if you'd really come or not."

I read a study once saying that the average adult laughs seventeen times a day, while a child laughs about three hundred times. Lorenzo was eighteen then, the same age I was, and I wondered what the statistics were for boys like us.

I looked at Lorenzo's earnest face, so open even in the half-light from the wet moon, shadows of leaves moving across his forehead.

I touched my chest, ribs on the surface, felt my heart underneath—contracting, releasing, I touched my forearm, picked at where the blood had dried, and winced remembering the thick brown belt, frayed at the edges, coming down again and again.

I could hear my father in my head: *This is for what you did. And this is for what you didn't do. This is for who you are. This is for who you aren't.*

Lorenzo sensed I was drifting away to somewhere else and hugged me so forcefully that all the air pushed out of my lungs. I was left limp like an empty bag. I let myself be held up.

"You don't have to go back there. Ever," he whispered. "Your father doesn't deserve you. Your mother either. And we can go back and get your sister. We can build a palace out of sticks and mud and live there together. The only rule will be: no acts of violence."

No more belts, no more fists, no more yelling, I thought.

I wasn't sure I should give myself this comfort, but I started thinking about Beaver Palace all the time. I pictured it like one of those geodesic dome houses crazy hippies in the desert like to build, but with all these interwoven sticks—each stick the exact right shape and size to fit. And then the river mud we'd paw on like adobe, and it would be so warm inside and heat up when even the smallest amount of sunshine broke through the clouds. On that day, alone with Lorenzo in Forest Park, I kissed him on the mouth and tried to let myself believe.

We tried living with some squatters in an abandoned building off East Burnside, but it was too wet, too cold, and too hard. We were too soft. I kept getting colds, then sinus infections: I just couldn't get warm. Lorenzo went back to his parents' house, I went back to mine, and it was better for a little while. Mom was glad I was home and she must have forced Dad to give me some space. But it went back to normal after about a month with the lectures and the disgust. No more belts, though, and no more fists—he had finally given up on that.

The best part of being home was seeing Buster every day. She really was a special, strange kid: tough and sweet and so funny. I wanted to tell her, "It's not your job to make this family function. You don't have to spend so much time trying to please everyone," but I didn't. I don't know why I didn't say something and I regret it now.

Even though it felt silly, I still thought a lot about Beaver Palace. It felt like a real place where we would finally be able to relax, to let our guards down, to not have to perform. Lorenzo would probably cry more, but not in a bad way. Every boy I knew forced themselves to suck it up, but for what? At Beaver Palace, Buster could be a kid and not have to fix everyone all the time. Me? I'd be more and more myself. I'd grow my hair out long and thick like I'd always wanted and my shoulders would relax and soften. I'd write songs on the guitar and play them in the evenings while the frogs in the river sang along. Even with this dream, I knew I had to go. When I took the pills and sliced my wrists, Beaver Palace was what I focused on with everything I had.

Lorenzo (Spring 2004)

It was my twenty-sixth birthday, so I went to the river alone like I always do. The water was wild and churning because of all the spring rain. My boyfriend Meyer had said he would take the day off work so we could do something together, but I had blown him off, said dinner together later would be plenty. I didn't even want to do that.

My parents each called and left a message. My dad talked about how he couldn't believe he was old enough to have a twenty-six-year-old because he thought he still had the qualities of someone that age himself, said something about not being ready to be a grandparent of all things, that his legs were still too nice to be that old. He talked about himself and how virile he was for a while more. My mom called and cried a little, called me her only baby, slurred. She has been nurturing a fondness for gin the past few years. The last time I saw her in person, the pores of her body gave off an acidic perfume.

What I wished for on my birthday, and wanted the most, was to cut all ties, to be alone, to move to some vast wilderness with only wild animals for company. I knew this looked bad from the outside, especially coming from a family of depressives in a city of depressives, so I was resisting. I wanted the quiet of it all, to not answer to anyone or pretend I felt things I didn't feel, and to sever ties with all the artifice, small talk, niceties, the appetizers and the entrees, the being polite and the being normal. I didn't even want to have sex anymore, preferring my beloved solitude.

Meyer had these good friends we often hung out with. All they wanted to talk about was having children and how they were working with one of Portland's best realtors to find their forever home (a term I despised, especially when they said it). Listening to them made my skin crawl. They were already insufferable, and they were about to be more so as parents and property owners. They possessed a kind of self-absorption that I understood from my parents, but also from myself. Depression is, unfortunately, very self-involved. I knew that I wasn't better than them—I was terrible in my own unique way. One night when everyone had had too much to drink, Meyer's friends started talking about a winter cruise to Jamaica and I couldn't take it anymore.

I said, "Do you know all the human excrement that ends up in the ocean thanks to the cruise ship industry? The horribleness of all us terrible Americans descending in a colonized port town? All the wasted resources. All the fucking germs. And everything is fake plastic shit made in China. It's fucking fake as fuck. Cruises are disgusting."

I wish I could just be friendly and go along with things, but it wasn't one of my strengths.

It was awkward after that to say the least, but Meyer made a joke and brought everyone what was left of a chocolate cake he had made the day before, hoping it would soak up all the liquor. We all pretended I hadn't just freaked out on them, which made me feel both better and worse.

They started talking about a remodeled Victorian for sale near Mt. Tabor. That's when I remembered Beaver Palace.

I drifted away from them, and pictured myself there so easily, with Neil and Buster. In my daydream, we'd spent the past eight years constructing our watery home, bending sticks and setting them just so, a kind of basket to hold us.

Neil (2004)

The day I killed myself (which feels like centuries ago) was the day I realized that if the only thing keeping me here was the fantasy of living with beautiful Lorenzo and my little sister in a beaver dam, I was pretty much fucked. The weight of things was overwhelming and I knew it wouldn't get better. I knew it somehow, in a deep, unavoidable way. So I did it, quickly, after putting it off for so long, and I was gone.

Even from here, I still think about Beaver Palace, those smooth branches, that warmth. I'll be here waiting, hoping Lorenzo lets himself fall in love and be loved over and over again until he's ancient. I'll watch Buster grow up, see all the amazing things she does. And I'll be busy too, collecting sticks and packing mud, preparing for their eventual arrival, keeping myself useful and busy—holding everything together for us just above the water, exactly where I'm supposed to be.

Tyranny of the Quantifiable

In the springtime—when the air warmed and smelled like sage and dirt cracked in protest—is when things started falling apart. We lived in a small, yellow house with a broken fence and a pine tree too weak to withstand my dreams of a treefort. So I sat underneath it in the backyard instead. I was eleven. My older brother Carter watched reruns and masturbated on the couch. His blank-eyed rhythmic pumping scared me, and my only way to cope was to stay away. Mom wasn't very helpful. I can picture her at the kitchen table arguing with whichever boyfriend was over.

She didn't date more than one person at a time, but the rotation was well established: honeymoon, anger, break up, back to a former boyfriend to give it another try. Repeat. Later when I was older and had sushi for the first time, sitting on a stool as the little boats passed, I thought of her own circular waterway: take what looks good, eat out of necessity, feel unsatisfied, still hungry, and look with a strange, nonsensical hope to the next boat coming down the chute. The bright green wasabi and the fleshy pink of ginger always started out so vivid, but with each time around the moat, the excitement of the colors faded.

That was the spring I started counting. Counting everything. How many times Mom looked me in the eye each day:

Average = 1. How many times Carter spoke to me without disdain: Average = 0. How many times I felt, in one of her boyfriend's side glances, that he wanted me gone: Average = 4. How many times I sat alone, back against the tree, feeling the weight of loss for something I didn't know how to name: Average = X. How do you count what feels like a constant?

I used a pocket knife, stolen from a cousin who lived across town, to make counting marks in the tree. The bark bled sap and smelled like family. The knife soon made it to my own bark, but my sap was red and flowed easier. I made my deepest cuts when the knife blade was sticky with sap: we were blood brothers. When the thin scabs disintegrated and the scars became quiet, milky rivers, I ran my hand over them and felt like something mattered. I was a living testimony to the uncountable.

By the time the marks made it up from ankle to knee, then thigh to hip, I was becoming too restless to sit quietly with my tree. Mom called Carter and me into the living room at the start of summer and told us she was getting married. She sat on her new boyfriend Gary's lap when she told us while the TV droned on behind them. I felt repulsed, but mostly angry with myself that I still cared enough to feel anything at all, much less betrayed.

The yard could no longer contain me after that. Years later, still roaming this wild country, displaced from the small, quiet forest I desired, I could feel the kindred sap flowing from veins to heart, pumping under bark, keeping me alive.

What the Ex Broke

My girlfriend Simone and I have only been dating for a little over a year. We met at a mutual friend's backyard dinner party, which felt very romantic and charming, as opposed to swiping a screen to find a lover. Not to be judgmental. Whatever it takes. As we had our first conversation, the river that ran past our friend's house glistened in the night and everything took on a momentous feel.

Her ex is a washed-up but diehard punk rocker. I know this because her son, Mateo, who is ten, talks about his dad constantly during the weeks he's with Simone. She's a clinical psychologist and has diagnosed her ex as a narcissist, fully aware that just about everyone throws this diagnosis around these days. In her case, she knows exactly what it entails and is not using the term lightly. On our third date, at a little Italian cafe downtown, she explained her theory—that her ex actively, though subconsciously, tries to convince his kid to idolize him by bombarding him with epic monologues on the subject of his own glory.

"He attempts to spin each of his many failures into a conquest, where every public slight he is forced to endure becomes the inspiration for a passionate soapbox speech about the personal injustices he experiences. Nothing, of course, is his responsibility," she sighed, before changing the subject.

According to Mateo, his dad cries at the end of every movie they watch, but also occasionally threatens to beat him with a leather belt. But then his dad just cries, never hits him, and promises fervently he never will. Mateo speaks adoringly of him even when explaining all this, which I think further confirms Simone's narcissist theory.

Simone is great because almost nothing is too precious to her and she doesn't believe that things should be sugarcoated. She lays it all out there in the open. When I first slept over, I went to the bathroom and the door knob fell off, then I noticed the whole door was completely knocked out of shape, hanging on the paint-peeled frame at a strange angle.

"Oh that," she said. "My ex broke it during one of his rages a few years ago."

She showed me how to put on and turn the door knob so it stayed in place, then we went back to bed and had more sex. We have a lot of sex when Mateo isn't around, almost none when he is. Week on, week off. It has become a rhythm between two extremes. What I've learned is things aren't very sexy when children are anywhere remotely nearby, even with the door locked late at night. Even when Mateo's running around the neighborhood and won't be back for hours, I can't do it. I'm not sure how to get over this. I jokingly started calling Mateo *the little cockblocker*, but not within earshot of course. Kids these days hear everything it seems, and the whole ugly, gorgeous world exposes itself to them in an onslaught.

At Saturday dinner last week, Mateo was going on and on in his little kid way. To be honest, neither of us were listening too closely because that kid has really mastered the art of the monologue, but he got our complete attention when we heard him say, "bukkake."

"What?!" we both gasped, thinking he got a word wrong from one of the old, grainy Japanese *Godzilla* movies he watches and rewatches with his dad.

But no, it turns out he knew exactly what bukkake is. That got us into a whole conversation with him about what he's seeing on the internet, how porn is not real sex, that it distorts and leaves things out, but he only just turned nine.

It's hard to know what exactly is getting in there when we talk to him. What can he understand with complexity, being so far removed from romantic love, from the foreign concepts of adult or even adolescent sexuality?

All this prompted a new rule of only being online in the living room, but it seems like a drop in the bucket. At a certain point, it's all just out of one's hands how a child is going to turn out, as painful as that is to admit.

Spending more and more time at their house, it has become clear many things have been broken: the handle on the refrigerator door, a wall in the laundry room, there's even a burnt area near the front entrance.

"It absolutely builds character," Simone says with a matter-of-factness that seems to be the work of many years of successful personal therapy, though I'm left unclear on whether she's talking about herself or the house.

Mateo's behavior increasingly concerns me, but I try not to say too much. Lately things haven't been going very well. There's nightly bed-wetting, ear-splitting tantrums, and steadily-growing egotism. At his soccer game just this afternoon he complained that no one passed to him, then started screaming his head off, erratically stumbling around the penalty area like a rabid dog.

"BUT I'M THE BEST!" he roared, right before storming

off the field in an astounding fit of rage, middle fingers stabbing the air, and spittle flying, "I'M THE FUCKING BEST!"

Witnessing moments like this throw me into an anxiety-infused, existential panic. Tonight after Mateo went to bed, Simone and I had a talk. I think she could tell I was upset by what happened at the soccer game. She tried to console me.

"If he's going to grow up to be a narcissist, he's going to grow up to be a narcissist," she said, shrugging.

Then she asked me what I think she should be doing differently with the first hint of defensiveness I've ever noticed in her voice.

"We're doing our best," she said, "and that is enough." She's probably right. She knows about things like this.

I haven't been sleeping well. I wake up with my stomach churning, sharp and acidic, thinking about Mateo getting older and bigger, and what he might do. I take a deep breath and try to calm down. I want so much to be more like Simone, to share her belief that everything will work out fine.

Over and over she tells me it's better not to hold anything too preciously.

"It's best to be in the moment, to stay calm and not get too worked up," she tells me, placing her warm hand on my tense back. I look down at my hands when she tells me this, trying to feel it, trying to believe.

FOREST

Look Up

When we were younger, Ramona and I (occasionally) partook in various recreational drugs, usually when we were avoiding the most genocidal of the Christian holidays, Thanksgiving and Easter. And sometimes on a birthday. And sometimes, well, when circumstances called for it. It has become a bit of a tradition.

Ramona is the kind of person who, with the slightest intoxicant, starts sort of glowing from her cells. Her smile grows wider than a shark's and she knows she's the shit. This knowing seems to last for weeks, or maybe that's just Ramona. It isn't in an egotistical way, it's more that she is special and she knows it, knows she is a human worth the space she takes up. I've always admired that about her. When I partook in the smallest amount of anything, I felt on top of the world for all of twenty minutes, then started chewing away at my own body, cuticles first, then nails, right before swan diving off a cliff of shame into despair. Not always, but often.

To each their own.

Ramona is the kind of person who everyone falls in love with, sooner or later, at least a little bit. Sometimes a lot. Back then, she drove a beat-to-hell Ford truck, Forest Service green, that hauled all her camping gear, surf gear, miscellaneous hunks of driftwood that rolled around the truck bed with each careening turn, and a few jars of preserved jams or pickled wild asparagus she'd harvested and canned herself as gifts for people she might encounter on her adventures, of which there were many. Having been friends for over twenty years, when we divorced our spouses within three months of each other, we decided to move in together. "Platonic partners," we called ourselves. She had many suitors. And they were usually kind and funny and smart, sometimes hot and sometimes a little dumb, which was fine. However long they lasted, I was glad to know she was being loved well, on her terms.

My friend Kaia, who I'd known since I was three years old, asked once if I was envious or jealous—she knew how fond I was of Ramona. I wasn't either of those things. I also had lovers sometimes, but I wasn't really interested in romancing or being romanced, at least not in any traditional sense. There was something else I wanted. Or maybe it was something else I already had, but couldn't recognize or grasp. I wasn't sure.

When our separations were finalized, Ramona and I converged in the middle, hauling cardboard boxes filled with our respective lives into an old, wind-beaten, two-story farmhouse she had inherited from her great-grandfather on the Oregon coast. We helped each other, did projects together, planted summer vegetable gardens together, fixed busted rain gutters together, cooked and ate countless meals together, and raised children together. We hugged and cried at weddings and funerals and sappy movies, and sometimes said cutting things we regretted—we had disagreements and worked them out and often rested our heads in the comforting lap of the other on the couch in the evenings. We said *good morning* and called each other *babe*, said *I'll miss you*, and *I'll make us dinner tonight, something extra good, what are you in the mood for?* and *hope you have good dreams.* We told each other we were cute and hot and funny and smart as hell even if we had just done something questionable. We told each other we were aging well. We told each other we had so much to offer, that we were good and whole. Sometimes we went out dancing with friends. Sometimes we danced in the living room—just the two of us—pajamas loose, hair a mess. We said *I love you* and meant it.

Her two older kids were beautiful, grown now, and they could easily have sailed through college with part-time modeling careers. And their brains! Each of them, magnificent. Their father was unimportant, as many are. More of a sperm donor. Sometimes it's better that way. My partner Essie and I had divorced because even though we loved each other we couldn't find a way to settle into getting along. She was beautiful and funny, but there was never any peaceful rest with us. It was always a fight and we had grown very tired. I had never been trying to prove anything to straight people, or anyone else, but it was still disappointing to fully understand that gay marriage can just as easily turn into gay divorce. We didn't have children but I still felt like I—we—had let someone down, someone besides us, but there was no one else.

Ramona's youngest child, Avery, had always held us in thrall by the scruff of our necks with her two strong little baby hands. We were weak before her, amazed and perturbed. I had known her since she was born, the fattest newborn I'd ever seen and by far the cutest. Rolls upon rolls that made all of our friends think she would be sturdy enough to make it in this world. That was what we all wanted then: to look upon a baby and know she had what it took to live as the Anthropocene started tanking.

Avery was all that and more. She was very...here. Her eye

contact alone was profound and disconcerting, better than any adults' I knew. Definitely better than mine. If I really concentrated, I could look into someone's eyes for about one minute, then I needed a break to recover. It was like Avery was born to make eye contact. I know this next part will sound like she was parentified or something, but she did this other thing: when we gave her hugs to comfort her, it was she who would lean in and pat our backs like we were the big babies, like we were the ones who needed comfort and she knew it.

She was also, you know, just a regular baby. She ate her smooshed-up carrots and pooped them out. She burped and cried and screamed and tried to torture the cat. Luckily the cat was smarter than all of us combined and the most agile, of course. Avery put the dust balls we hadn't swept up yet in her mouth, coughed, and spat them out. She watched the birds and the deer when they came through the yard in one of their many crusades to annihilate the flowers Ramona planted in the old pasture. Avery sat in the grass and laughed in the sun. She crawled out into the rain and looked up and let the drops hit her perfect, little, round face.

The troubling thing, though, was that even before she could properly walk, she could climb trees. While the rest of her was fat, her little baby arms were freakishly muscular like a chimpanzee's. I can't describe in words how incomprehensibly horrifying it is to see a human baby perched in the limbs of a tall, crooked shore pine, out of reach. The first time it happened, I started taking these deep breaths like I might just die if I didn't focus on breathing, while Ramona launched into action, pulling a dusty trampoline to where Avery sat high above. Next, she ran to find an old extension ladder because the thing was, there were no low branches we could reach to climb up to her, just bare trunk. *How the fuck did she get up there?* As I continued to take deep breaths, I was able to watch Avery closely—everything in slow motion, just like people talk about while a trauma is unfolding.

She wobbled a bit, but it was clear she was in complete control. She scooted herself down the branch a little, right above where I stood on the trampoline, still stress-breathing. She made the most exquisite eye contact with me, smiled her perfect baby smile, cawed like a young crow and fell backwards into my arms. Ramona saw the whole thing. She ran over and we all hugged and cried with relief, Avery between us, patting our sweaty backs to let us know we were silly to have been so worried.

We never did figure out how she shimmied up tree trunks because even when we thought we were being sneaky by hiding in the bushes (yes, both of us, several times) or behind an upstairs curtain or through a crack in the front door, she knew when we were watching and wouldn't go anywhere near any of the trees. We even got one of those trail cams set up outside. Still, no dice. This was not a secret she was going to let us in on. It was after Avery escaped once late at night, over her crib bars and down the stairs, out the door and up into a young maple with skinny branches that could have broken—that we put fence posts and chicken wire around each tree on the property, of which there were hundreds. In the meantime we tried to keep an eye out, but Avery always found a way. With time, we became less disturbed—were really just more in awe. A prodigal climber? Was she an arborist savant?

Eventually, our nervous systems calmed. We would find her in a tree, call whoever was in the house to come look: there she was! Out on a branch, sniffing the air and rubbing sap onto her shirt. We learned to delight in this thing that had once so terrified us. There was the sound she made when she was ready to come down, the same sound she had cawed out the first time. One of us would position ourselves beneath her and just like that first time, she would plop backwards into our arms, no fear.

As she grew older, she stopped climbing trees, and when asked about what she remembered from that year, she said it was all a bit fuzzy and changed the subject. We tried to respect her privacy.

Avery would be leaving us soon, eighteen now with a full scholarship to study in Prague for four years. We'd always guessed that when she flew away, she would fly far, it was just how she was.

Ramona and I sat on the porch a lot during those years. Even after so much time passed together, after many small and large traumas of life had befallen us, and possibly too much time together, I couldn't help but be a little in love with her. I didn't want to kiss her and I didn't not want to kiss her, it still wasn't about that at all. I wanted to be her friend in a different kind of way, maybe an unprecedented way in the history of friendships. I knew it was naive to even think of such a thing as this: the idea that our friendship had to be the only one of its kind in the history of civilization to be special or meaningful. I intellectually knew that wasn't it. I knew that even just a normal friendship could be profound. The thing was, even though we'd known each other for so long, I didn't feel like we'd totally let each other in. There was a distance between us that disoriented me.

I called Kaia, and she reminded me that I had always been like this.

"Remember when you used to send me roses when I had my internship in Brooklyn for a summer?" she'd asked. "They were like a hundred bucks for each bouquet delivered and you were a broke-ass bike messenger then. What did you have to give up for yourself to pay for that? Dinners for a week? And it wasn't just expensive stuff, it was like you were courting me in so many other little ways, even though I've known you my whole life."

"Okay, but is that so weird?" I asked, but of course I knew exactly what she meant.

I could hear her take a deep breath on the other end of the line. "It's just...unnecessary. We, your close friends, already know you love us. I know it. Ramona knows it. Everyone knows it. You're a great lover of your friends."

I let this sink in. I could understand what she was saying but that's not how it felt. What about all the stupid things I'd said, year after year, how I'd failed them in small ways, maybe large ways I wasn't even aware of, and what about the times I said too much or said too little? What about when I was judgmental or too needy or too sincere or just an asshole? It felt like a lot.

The thing is, I actually liked very few people. It was about once every nine years I met someone I really liked. Even during the years I was with Essie, with all the sex and intimacy and depth I could ever want, this other kind of friendship still felt like an achy desire, just not one that emanated from the genitals. It wasn't lust. It was this thing that I didn't know if other people even felt. It was like everyone else had an understanding about what a friend was and what that meant and I was on the outside still trying to figure it out. Kaia would have told me, if I'd asked, that I was trying too hard.

"Can't friendships be like this—one of the most special things?" I'd asked Kaia.

"You tell me," she said, leaving me hanging with no clear

answers and no obvious course of action. Later that night, I fought the urge to go out into the moonlight to pick a bouquet of flowers for Kaia, then drive the six hours to her house in Portland to leave them on her doorstep with a love note.

The next morning, Kaia texted me something her therapist had told her.

"What if you do nothing?"

I didn't like how that sounded and replied, "Hmm. Something to think about."

Who was I if I wasn't a person to take some kind of action? I was afraid of my lack of action being misinterpreted, but also afraid my actions would be misinterpreted as well. Do nothing? My very resistance made me know she was onto something.

Over the next few months, I practiced doing nothing and it was easier than I imagined. Maybe because there was nothing to do except to continue to be with Ramona and Avery too, keep existing together, keep showing up—to see what was happening, what would happen next, and to tell stories about what had already happened. Forever, maybe, if I was lucky.

At breakfast on a bright Sunday morning, Ramona leaned towards me across our slab of kitchen table, worn and oiled by time, "Everything okay with you? You've been kind of quiet lately."

"I'm trying to do nothing," I said. "Kaia suggested I try it."

"But, what are you trying not to do?" she asked. "Are you struggling with something?"

I wanted to let it all out then, about the ache that wasn't describable, that I thought no one would understand. I wondered if there was a name for this in some other language, this desire for intimacy that wasn't sexual. Maybe in Tagalog, or maybe in

German somehow. Like how they had all these words that don't exist in English. My favorite was Verschlimmbessern—when you try too hard to fix something and end up making it even worse.

I thought back to the times we had partaken in mind-altering substances, how much liminal space got created, and how free we had felt to move around, emotionally, as well as in our bodies, bones and muscle suddenly so loose and light. Psychedelics weren't profoundly interesting to me in and of themselves, but I liked how they made time feel larger.

Instead of explaining any of this I said, "I really miss when Avery used to climb the trees." I hadn't really thought about that in years. "I miss when we used to look up to a complete spectacle, and how strange and special it was, like it was just for us, that it's what made us a family somehow."

"I miss it too," Ramona said. She didn't cry often, but her eyes were glistening now. "It was like, I don't know how to describe it, like we were here to…" she dropped off.

"Yeah," I said, tears also welling. "What *was* that?" I asked.

"I think she reminded us to look up," Ramona said, after a moment. "And once the fear subsided, to be delighted."

It came out before I could stop myself.

"I'm most delighted when I look at you," I said.

I immediately regretted it, even though it was true. I felt like I might actually throw up. After all these years, I still feared she would retreat if I told her how I really feel about her.

But she surprised me, even though there was really no reason to be surprised: we had been through it all. I realized this is what Kaia had meant.

Ramona took a moment. "I feel the same. Let's keep doing that. Looking and being delighted, for as long as we possibly can."

Outside the trees had no babies in them, but they swayed in the wind as their branches creaked. They were making a symphony, just for us, as they had all along.

Ramona held out her hand to me, and I took it.

King

Manny wanted a snake for his tenth birthday but I didn't think I could handle it.

"What do you think about a hamster instead? Or a rabbit or a guinea pig?" I asked. "A kitten?"

I hoped to sway him towards some kind of mammalian creature, something with fur and emotive eyes, something I could actually love. But Manny kept insisting, week in and week out. I'd never known him to be so determined. After many tearful pleas, a stack of library books that he checked out on his own about caring for snakes, and an earnest handwritten letter left under my pillow promising nightly dishwashing and lawn mowing until he turned eighteen, I gave in.

The day before his birthday we drove down to Ashland's Reptile Room, a warehouse staffed by a paunchy middle-aged man with creepy facial hair and two sulky teenage goths with metal in their lips.

"Oh!" Manny yelled after five minutes of running down the aisles of tanks in a frenzied mania. "This is the one. Look at him!"

I looked.

The snake was two feet long with a wide spade for a head. Its body had a wavy, black and brown pattern that looked like a Rorschach Test. Its empty eyes darted mechanically. I called to the goth who was lurking at the end of the aisle to see if she could tell us more about it. She sauntered over.

"This one requires live mice weekly, little ones called pinkies." She stared out at us from under her black bangs.

The mice were an unexpected reality I found appalling. I looked at Manny to see what he thought about it.

"Cool!" Manny said, trying to make eye contact with the snake.

As usual, I did not want to say no to Manny. I found myself lacking the strength even to haggle him down to a smaller snake, a cricket-eating one. When I was a child, all I ever heard was *no* to this and *no* to that. I didn't care about toys so much but it seemed to me that every interest I had, every desire, was dismissed with some kind of refusal. I'd always wanted to be the type of person to give a resounding *yes*—to myself, and also to my son. I wanted to say *yes* to living, to the things that pushed me, or even scared me. I thought this one word would make being alive more exciting, more meaningful. I wanted to be that person, with that life.

"I'm naming him King," Manny declared, his damp forehead pressed against the glass. "I love him already."

I smiled, willing myself to match his enthusiasm, because even though I didn't want to say no, I also really didn't want the snake. I set myself aside and thought of Manny, then took a deep breath and started packing the aquarium, a bag of garish pebbles, a large stick with fake leaves, and a book titled *Herp Husbandry* into the cart. By the time we drove back across town and into our driveway, I was already fantasizing about exactly how and when I could get rid of my son's new pet.

When Manny went to his father's house on the weekends, my boyfriend Owen would come over. Owen worked in finance doing something so tedious I didn't have the patience to fully understand. Investment something. Manny's father and I broke up when Manny was two, and though I had dated several people since then, Owen had somehow lasted the longest—though he wasn't the kindest, as I had initially hoped. I thought his outdoorsy hobbies (rock climbing and sailing) and his bright-faced tan meant he had his life together, but when he drank, he became violent and the ugly things inside him were forced to the surface. The best thing to do, I'd learned, was to wait it out, leave the house, or get a book and earplugs and lock the bathroom door. I'd spent many evenings sitting in the bathtub until the storm of him passed, as if he was a hurricane, a weather pattern that would eventually shift. There was no reasoning with Owen when he got this way, but if I could find a way to leave him alone, he usually didn't strike.

When sober, Owen was easy and low-key. He thought it was hilarious when he came over and saw I had given in to Manny's snake idea, knowing how much I would struggle with the mice. But he wouldn't do it either.

"I'm a vegan!" he exclaimed. "Just being in the same room with that thing is already compromising my core values."

I looked at Owen closely—really saw him, through his white teeth and his warm skin, maybe for the first time. He was another boy to take care of—a child, but in a bigger, older body. He was all exuberance, but no substance. In that glance, I saw he couldn't be counted on—sober or not—to hold me steady. I would always be the one doing the holding. Still, I knew I wanted to say yes to him. I also knew I'd have to deal with Manny's snake—and all the other things that would surely come—on my own.

I could have waited. The snake would have survived without

a mouse until Manny got back from his dad's. But looking at King, locked away for life in a glass case, it was him who I felt compassion for. I imagined that catching and eating the mouse might offer him some relief from his captivity, from his monotonous nothingness.

I had a strong sense the pink, baby mouse knew what was coming when I scooped her up and set her down. I watched and waited, sick to my stomach, feeling like a Satanist.

"I'm going out to get some drinks for tonight!" Owen yelled from the living room. I heard the screen door slam behind him before I could answer, asking him not to.

I turned back to the aquarium just in time to see the mouse's back feet slip past King's open throat, and I thought of Manny, and boyhood, and responsibility, and I thought of myself, hiding behind doors, and the exhausting harshness of love, and I knew in that moment that King—sliding along the plastic leaves, tongue flickering, demanding things of me I didn't have the capacity for—would stay.

I Am Right Here

I always thought everything was more easily learned by children than by those of us in our advanced years, but it turns out that is not exactly true. At my latest lesson my piano teacher Sasha let me know I'm progressing significantly quicker than her young pianists, and that I'm her favorite student. I found it so endearing and felt a burst of ardent emotion, something I hadn't experienced in ages. If I was forty years younger, I would certainly ask her to go on a date with me, but regrettably I am no longer up for anything remotely resembling a date. Sometimes I look in the mirror and get a bit of a shock, staring at my reflection and asking it, "What the hell happened to you?" Unfortunately, I already know the answer so I don't bother responding.

The children she teaches must be feeble-minded because it's hard to imagine I can outshine them. I get so nervous sitting there next to Sasha. My hands shake, and songs I practiced perfectly at home alone are jittery and rushed when I perform them for her. That's not the age, that's the feelings. Sasha is from Kiev and was taught by stern Ukrainian music teachers who pinched her arms sadistically for missed notes or mediocre posture, demanding perfection. It's astonishing that anyone taught in that traditional way continues to want to have anything to do with a piano, but I think Sasha is resilient. Picture a forest elf sitting on a piano bench with a mischievous smile, playing gorgeous pieces to demonstrate certain techniques, making insightful comments, and blushing occasionally. That's Sasha. You'd be enchanted by her too.

I take lessons at the Russian School of Piano and Musical Theory, where the waiting room is filled with loud, little brats who have no idea how privileged they are to learn an instrument in their youth. I'm the oldest one in the waiting room by at least seven decades, blending into the beige walls until the door to Room Five opens and Sasha welcomes me in.

Sometimes near the end of the lesson we close the cover of the piano and talk for a few minutes about philosophy, history, or just life. We have to do it in secret because, even at my age, if the director saw anything other than the strictest of lessons taking place, Sasha is convinced she'd be fired. Fortunately it's not too hard to steal these minutes since the director is often busy yelling at unambitious children. Sometimes Sasha even locks the door and I feel a secret thrill, as though we are in on something together. Once during one of these conspiratorial moments I told her about going to southern Sicily years ago.

"I unexpectedly heard the call to prayer for the first time and burst into tears."

She leaned in and I continued, "The rich sound tapped into some ancient part of myself, cellular. I've never forgotten it."

Then she told me about how Beethoven used to submerge his entire head in cold water before composing, and how his last words were, "Plaudite, amici, comedia finita est." Applaud, my friends, the comedy is over.

"Some people deny these were his last words," Sasha said, "but I choose to believe."

I adore that concept, about choosing to believe—the subjective nature of reality. So we discussed that. Our conversations are quite far-reaching, connecting seemingly separate ideas and realities into an extensive, living nexus of understanding. No one really knows how to have conversations like this anymore. People just parrot back what they hear on the news with incredulity at the latest political headlines, but hardly anyone really seems to want to make the requisite effort to think, feel, or discuss deeply.

At our lesson last week she asked me to put my hand on top of hers so I could really feel the difference between staccato and legato, not just hear or see it. Her hand was a lot cooler than mine, and her skin was smooth, whereas mine was dry and weathered. My heart beat like a wild stampede, sitting so close, and—in a sense—getting to hold her hand.

There's this thing that has started happening, sometimes late at night when I can't sleep, sometimes in the middle of the day. I can feel myself disappearing at the edges, and sense the end is finally near. I am not on my deathbed. I still walk the six blocks to my piano lesson each week, but what you need to understand is I don't imagine I'm going to die in a slow, deathbed kind of way. I'm going to go out quickly, like an ember extinguished by a sharp gust of wind. This has always been what I wanted, and I knew when it was time, I could make it so. I've done a lot of research about how to leave when I'm ready. I don't like the word suicide—that's for young people. At my age, I like to think of it as making a rational choice simply to depart slightly sooner than I would otherwise.

The main song I've been practicing on the piano is "я прямо здесь," which translates to "I Am Right Here." When I play it I feel this sense of exquisite calm, and I feel how easy it would be to just let go. Let it all go. Let life go is what I mean. This song makes me not afraid of doing so, and spreads a warmth through my body. I felt that once I could play this song all the way through, it would be time.

Because I was getting close, I decided to tell Sasha about the emotions she inspired in me. It wasn't about romance, it was about the feeling underneath romance, where I'd always held the suspicion something even richer existed. I didn't expect her to understand. However, I hoped somehow that my words would matter to her.

At the end of my last lesson, I played "я прямо здесь" all the way through—not perfectly, but with full presence. She smiled at me and put her hand on my back, congratulating me. With our remaining time, we listened to an Erik Satie song we both loved, and I looked at her radiant face and felt the most beautiful kind of sadness, the exquisite kind you can't bear to turn away from. Then the clock struck five and my time was up. I opened the door to the waiting room, and turned back in her direction. Strangled with sudden hoarseness, I whispered, "I feel so much for you."

In a nightmarish slow motion I realized with dismay that she hadn't heard me, and I could not bear to repeat myself. Her next student, a five-year-old with a ghastly cough, had barged into the room yelling at his distraught mother, who was trying to usher him towards Sasha's piano. Lost in this inane shuffle, I caught one last glimpse of Sasha. Her eyes were shining bright, and for a split second she was looking right at me as if nothing else existed, but I had no way of knowing if she had understood what I'd tried to convey.

I walked back home, sheet music tucked under my arm, not caring if it got wrinkled. The light in the street shined harshly, saturated with disappointment. I tried to let back in that idea of Sasha's I had so adored, that I could choose to believe something, and make it true. But on this last day, that concept—once so palpable—now felt impossibly far away. I thought about Beethoven's last words, looked up at the trees—starting to turn so green now—and walked home, humming the melody of "I Am Right Here" to myself.

Just This

My friend Jordan, who is a harm reduction counselor, explained with utmost seriousness that Sophie and I needed to get some lube and put the capsules up our butts.

"Wayyy up, Arlo, I mean it," Jordan said. "Otherwise it'll really itch. It bypasses the digestive system that way, straight to the bloodstream."

We did as we were told.

Nervous at first, then giddy, we walked to the old cemetery, laid down and gazed upwards, suddenly euphoric in the present moment. It was such a relief. The trees were fucking majestic. The other few humans there, off in the distance, were endearing; they looked like little hobbits with misshapen bodies, doing nonsensical things with their arms and legs. It was okay, all the silly things the humans were doing. Everything was okay.

Hours later, when the drugs wore off, we meandered home and nothing felt pressing anymore. We didn't even crash as we had been warned. We didn't get the sads. Things were just normal again.

A few nights later, I had drinks with my friend Thomas. He always complains about his home life, though he loves his wife and kids. They'd decided to have five children and I am genuinely sympathetic. The oldest is nineteen and a lazy mooch, the youngest is seven and prone to daylong temper tantrums, impossible to soothe.

Thomas had scotch waiting for me at the bar.

"It's been at least five years since we were all in a good mood at the same time," he said, looking morose.

I often think Thomas is gay and has gone over the top with all this baby making to prove a point. Something about performing straightness, something very 1950s. Everyone in his family is Orthodox Christian—Eastern Oregon homesteaders going back three generations. His decisions make sense to me in a strange way, even if they could have been avoided.

Sophie and I are non-monogamous. We also both identify as pansexual, a word that still makes me think of a mythical beast playing a flute whenever I say it out loud. Occasionally Thomas asks about the details, how either of us are okay with the other having sex with a stranger or an acquaintance.

"I'm not sure," I told Thomas. "It's just how it worked out."

I could tell my answer was unsatisfactory to him but wasn't sure what kind of details he wanted—if my sharing would make him feel better or worse about his own circumstances. A few months ago, a night when Thomas had gotten extraordinarily drunk, he'd asked me if he'd ever been on my list for a fling.

"I don't have a list," I told him, evading the question, and Thomas dropped it.

I looked over at him as he ordered us another round, but I was thinking of the trees, how tremendous they looked that day in the cemetery. And the people doing people things—just strange little creatures, all of us. I thought of Sophie and the way her face glowed in the sun, reflecting so much emotion. I've never told Thomas that we've been trying unsuccessfully to have a baby. We always play it off as if a child would hamper our life of adventure. It's not an outright lie. This has always been part of our conversations, but it's not the whole truth.

"Try to enjoy the adventure you're on," I told Thomas that night. "I'm sure there's never a dull moment at your house, unlike at ours. The highlight of my week was looking at a tree."

"That does sound pretty boring," he said, fumbling with the coaster, finally smiling a little.

I thought about the guy I had been with a couple months ago, how lonely I'd felt with him, like he wasn't really there at all and it was just me in that tacky hotel room off the 101 wondering—as I felt the dull thrusting of him—when the thick curtains had last been washed.

Jordan had given Sophie and me enough pills for two trips, and I thought about giving one of the pills to Thomas, to let him feel how splendid and delightful the world could be, if only for a few hours. But I knew I wanted to keep this for me and Sophie, a respite from all the external adventure—a quiet moment inside myself with the human I'd chosen and no sads. Just some trees, just this.

For the Birds

In an unexpected fit of cleaning, Grandma Mona found the German sewing scissors passed down from her deceased mother, Tanta, who died in the Oregon State Mental Hospital at age thirty seven.

"I've been looking for these for decades!" she cried out, grinning at me as she returned to her favorite living room chair to admire the scissors' sheen.

I watched her check the sharpness with her thin-skinned index finger and when she noticed I was paying such close attention, she gave me a wink and tried to send me to Ledger's with five dollars to get her some Tanqueray and tonic. She thinks she has a deal worked out with the owner that any child she knows can pick up alcohol for her with no questions asked, and that five dollars is enough for what she wants and then some.

"Get yourself some candy with the change, Lucy," she said, like I'm still a baby even though I'll be a freshman in high school next year. Everyone thinks I'm younger than I am and I'm beginning to think that trying so hard to be good is part of the problem.

Mom bought a few bottles of gin that she keeps in the basement for when Grandma Mona tries to send me or my younger brother Sebastian to the store. Mom learned in an elder care class that it's better to go along with whatever the old person's story is, instead of jostling them into reality.

Grandma Mona came to live with us last year after she burned her house down on accident. She bought a pack of cigarettes "just to try" because she never smoked and said she'd always wanted to see what all the fuss was about before she kicked the bucket. Her words.

She probably took a puff, choked out one of her shrill *goddamns*, and set down the cigarette to get a glass of water to wash away the nicotine taste. The abandoned cigarette tipped itself onto the old 1970s carpet and sent her little home up in a whoosh. That's the picture the fire chief painted for us as we stood around her blackened chimney afterwards. Everything besides the one corner room where her trunk was kept had burned down to the gray ash at our feet.

Sebastian has been obsessed with that fire chief ever since, keeps wanting to send him cards to say thank you for helping Grandma Mona. Mom already told him that one thank you card was enough. Mom thinks it's because he wants to be a firefighter too—all muscled and strong, his biceps popping when he lifts so much as a pencil. Sebastian starts eighth grade next year and currently comes in at about seventy-nine pounds fully dressed with a thick, leather belt and his heaviest pair of shoes.

Sebastian does not want to be a firefighter. Sebastian is one-hundred percent gay and doesn't give any shits about putting out flames, probably just wants to start some with any nice, handsome man that comes along, and the fire chief is all that and more. He seems to like older guys the best, though I did catch him eyeing a fellow middle school boy at Fancy Freeze the other day when we went for milkshakes. Not that he's done anything with anyone yet, but his proclivities are so obvious. Mom's oblivion seems to be an act of willful determination.

When high school starts in a few weeks, my friend Olivia will be going into her junior year. Since she's two years older than me, I'm hoping she'll tell me which teachers to try and avoid and which parties to crash. No more mister nice guy and no one to please but myself. Olivia and I met in Girl Scouts and we both dropped out after one year. Her dad wouldn't let her quit before giving it a real try and I stayed on to keep her company until he gave in.

"This is the most boring shit I've ever done," she said, after a long panel discussion with female entrepreneurs in the back room of the downtown library. Olivia turned to look at me while a middle-aged lady shared how empowering it had been for her to invest in the stock market as a younger woman. While the woman elaborated, Olivia slowly drew her finger across her pale throat and made a garbled choking sound while her green eyes rolled dramatically into the back of her skull. Later at Olivia's, sitting on her faded bedspread, I asked her if she felt bad that everyone probably saw her pretend to sever her own jugular, but Olivia frowned and told me that sometimes she really does cut herself.

"I mean, not my neck of course. Just my arms. It helps release all the bad stuff, makes me feel like I can handle things," she said, waving her arm around as if to point out all the invisible miseries surrounding us even now.

I wanted to know what the bad stuff was about but didn't want to ask—probably about her mom who she never talked about.

"How do you do it, like, without killing yourself by accident?" I asked.

She looked at me for a long moment like she was deciding on something, and then swung her sneakered feet to the other side of her bed and opened the top drawer of her nightstand. Taped to the underside was a pack of razor blades wrapped in thin cardboard. She led me into the bathroom and locked the door even though no one else was home. She lives with her dad, who is a handyman by day and a janitor at the community college at night. I've only met him once and—second to Mom—he was the most exhausted looking person I'd ever seen. My main takeaway from these observations is that I'm never, ever getting married and absolutely not having any children either. A life-suck, all of it.

Olivia washed her hands with antibacterial soap and dried them carefully.

"You've got to be really careful or things can get infected," she told me.

Her bare arms were beautiful and smooth with just a few scars here and there, not something I would have noticed. I leaned forward from where I sat on the edge of their clawfoot bathtub and reached out to touch those cold marks, carefully feeling the raised relief on the map of her.

When I looked up, she was watching me with a strange look on her face.

"I never thought I'd do this in front of anyone," she said.

She took a deep breath and held the razor at an angle. With all her focus, she drew blood to the surface in a clean red line. Then it spilled over—a thin trail running down her white, hairless arm. When I looked at her face, she was paler than usual and her eyes were closed, the razor resting in her open palm.

"I can't explain it, but it just feels like such a relief," she said after taking a deep breath, coming back to me.

She patted her arm clean with a cold washcloth and held it there for a few minutes. When she lifted it, I could see it had already started to seal itself up, to heal.

Back at home, I watched Sebastian cleaning his Chuck Taylors with a toothbrush dipped in dish soap. He doesn't know why Dad left us, but I do. Sebastian was too young when it happened, barely five, and Mom hasn't had it in her to correct the story she made up to get through those awful days.

"Your father could have lied and explained it away," she told me—not right then, but when I was a little older and pressed her for details, "but he didn't. He at least had the decency to feel ashamed and leave us without a big fight."

Dad had taken Sebastian into the shower and when Mom popped her head in to ask if they were hungry for dinner, she saw Dad doing something to Sebastian that no parent should do to a child.

Dad moved all the way across the country to Maine, said he was offered a job he couldn't refuse working on a lobster boat. For a while he sent us postcards with cartoon fishermen saying things like, *Fish you were here!* but those stopped after the first season. Sebastian keeps the ones addressed to him paperclipped together in the back of his desk, but I took mine to the backyard and burned them one by one, then washed the soot off my hands and tried to forget.

The new school year starts in a few days. I haven't seen Olivia since she showed me how she slices herself. She still posts pictures of herself on social media, so I know she's alive and having the time of her life while not texting me back.

Grandma Mona keeps her prized scissors right by her favorite chair and opens and closes them for hours while she watches

TV. Mom thinks they remind her of her mother—of the good times that involved bright fabric and sewing, before Tanta lost her marbles and was taken away from her forever.

With Grandma Mona taking a nap in her bedroom and no one else at home, I pick up the scissors, feel their cold weight, easily as sharp as Olivia's razor blades. In the upstairs bathroom with the door locked, I make the same preparations. I can see the draw of this, the solitary ritual of it, each step important. At first, when I open up the scissors and slide the edge across my skin, it looks like it didn't cut through, but then a long line of blood seeps out in slow motion and I feel a pressure relieve itself in me. It's like Dad's terrible shame, Mom's tired detachment, Sebastian's need for something I can't help him with, and my own fears about being a good person or not being a good person all come to the surface and drip away, leaving me lighter.

I clean up carefully, wipe the scissors, and set them back by Grandma Mona's chair like nothing ever happened. I take a shower and stick a bandage on my arm, change into a tank top, and put on a long sleeved shirt over that. The afternoons are starting to get cooler now so no one will suspect anything.

It's Sebastian who finds the first little pile later that evening, looking for an old set of Dad's thirty-pound weights in the front room that no one uses anymore. It used to be his office, before he got caught being a pedo and left us. Maybe Sebastian wants to be a chiseled firefighter after all. He's standing in the corner by the closet and looking down with a strange expression on his face.

"What. The. Fuck," he says slowly, reaching down and letting something move through his fingers, like sprinkling coarse salt over his dinner.

"Oh god," I say when I go over to him, take in what he's seeing.

Mom comes in and walks over. It takes her a minute too.

That's when we hear Grandma Mona in the downstairs bathroom that only she uses. Mom took the lock off when she first moved in in case there was ever some kind of emergency.

We follow as Mom knocks on the door and opens it without waiting, and there is Grandma Mona with her prized scissors, standing naked from the waist down, legs parted over the bathroom tile, being careful with the pink genitalia beneath her wild, untamed forest. Another small pile was forming below her, just like the one in the office, shimmering silver in the bathroom's harsh, overhead light.

Grandma Mona yells at Mom to *shut the goddamn door*, that this is her *goddamn private business* and we can all *go to goddamn hell*, but we all just stand there frozen, watching her snip her remaining pubic hairs away.

"It's for the birds! For their nests!" she screeches now. "It's something Mother used to do. She taught me. You should have seen all the birds' nests that were made with her help, you should have seen…"

She trails off; her pale, little butt all out in the open like a deflated birthday balloon.

"Let's gather this all up and set it outside for them," I say.

The look Grandma Mona gives me is made of such pure relief I think she might start crying. I take off my long-sleeve and scoop all the hairs up in it while Mom takes the scissors away and helps Grandma pull up her underwear and pants.

I gather up the pile in the office as well, and Sebastian and I go out into the part of the yard where Grandma can see us from the large back window, out under the summer string lights we haven't taken down yet. We look to the dark night sky and sprinkle her pubic hairs over the plants, drape the slightly longer strands over higher branches. We call the birds to us with our minds, willing them to understand, to use this offering.

When I shake out the remaining little hairs from my shirt, Sebastian notices my arm but doesn't say anything. The bandage has fallen off, revealing the long line across my upper forearm. We meet eyes.

"Put the long sleeved shirt back on before we go in," he says, and he sounds much older than he is, like he became a person who knows important things the second I stopped paying close attention.

I decide to go over to Olivia's without texting first. I am tired of her long silence and want to know where she's gone. Her dad answers the door, looking slightly less tired than usual.

"Hi Lucy," he says. "She's upstairs."

When I knock on her bedroom door she knows it's me and doesn't look surprised. I'm just wearing my t-shirt and her eyes go to the line on my arm immediately, like she was expecting as much.

"I don't do that anymore," she says. "My dad got laid off so he is around all the time now and he'd notice."

I nod, wishing I had worn my long sleeve shirt to cover myself up like Sebastian suggested.

"I have a pet leech now," she tells me. "I saw it on TikTok. It's like, you know, harm reduction."

I don't understand what she's telling me, so she goes over to her closet and brings out a jar filled with water and a piece of cheesecloth rubber-banded over the top.

"His name is Albert," she explains. "He just lives in this jar. He only has to feed once a year, but I feed him more than that. He doesn't make a big scar or anything, just sucks the blood out and leaves a tiny mark in the shape of a Y. I just fed him yesterday, otherwise I'd show you."

She hands me the jar and I look at Albert—a fat, thick blob attached to a rock at the bottom. Something dark and slippery slides through my intestines.

"Are you ready for school?" I ask, handing the jar back to her, not knowing what else to say.

"I think so," she says. "I can give you a ride if you want. Dad says I can use his car until he gets another job lined up."

"Cool," I say. "Thanks."

When I get home, Mom and Sebastian are cutting vegetables outside by the grill for a late dinner, soaking up the last bit of dwindling warmth from this long season.

"We are probably all going to end up seriously demented," Sebastian is saying to Mom, laughing a little. "It seems to run in the family."

"It's called *having dementia*," Mom corrected, pretending to be terse, "not *being demented*. It sounds even more messed up when you say it like that."

I walk towards them wondering if Mom will ever let herself fall in love again, wondering if Sebastian misses Dad or if he only thinks of the fire chief or the Fancy Freeze boy now, or if he occupies himself with other people and things I have no idea about. I wonder if Olivia will really show up to take me to school, if I will let myself do the things I've imagined—the not-good things I've pictured: sneaking cigarettes, giving hand jobs, and trying some sips of Grandma Mona's gin—trying to live a somewhat more compelling life.

"We are definitely all demented," I call out as I approach them, their faces turning towards me, my lone voice rising up the tops of the tallest trees. They join me then, our three voices cracking and unsure, but willing.

"We're all demented!" we shout together, Grandma Mona inside, hopefully sleeping soundly and proud of having put her mother's scissors to good use.

We throw our heads back as the sound lifts from our chests and throats, our eyes looking upwards for little birds with streaks of curled silver hanging from their beaks, making all their gorgeous plans.

The Sheet

Everyone was drunk, and then Henry pulled down his pants, dancing in his boxer briefs. It's a thing he does at parties sometimes. He thinks it's hilarious in the moment. This morning when he finally gets out of bed, he looks slightly embarrassed, but will not apologize. Henry never says sorry, he just keeps moving forward.

After a stretch and a big yawn, he says to the ceiling, "There were some real assholes at the party last night."

We met on our first day at college—art school in Portland. We both had bleached hair and looked miserable—two boys unable to hold eye contact—but I knew he liked me right away. Even when sad, he has a mischievous look I still can't turn away from. We had sex that night.

I told him, "You're never going to penetrate me, but I'm up for anything else."

He was fine with it. Over the years he's had sex with other people when he needs certain things, and so have I. The first time I saw him do that thing with his pants, I asked him why, and he told me it's almost like a compulsion—he's always chasing the moment when people's bright faces turn in his direction, even at his own expense. He started doing it in high school, and getting older has not made him want to stop.

Personally, I'd rather do everything from behind a curtain. I want to delight people, but don't want any recognition for having done so. In the high school theater class I joined (because there was another boy I liked in it) I was only willing to do sound or costumes—absolutely nothing could get me on stage. Even when I was a little kid and was asked which superpower I'd want, I said without pause, *invisibility*. My classmates wanted to know what kinds of crazy shit I'd do, who I'd spy on, and what I'd try to get away with.

"I just want people to stop fucking looking at me," I said. No one knew what to say after that.

It's been many years and I've never let Henry in. He thought I'd acquiesce, but eventually accepted it, and stopped asking. Sometimes though, I fantasize about being draped in a sheet like a woman from a cult or something, with just a dick hole in the middle, and letting him do it that way. I don't tell him this because he'd either be confused or too enthusiastic.

Tonight we are going to a friend's fundraiser with an open bar and it's likely that three drinks in, Henry will have his pants down. I will smile, pretend it's funny. We're separate people, but over time, there's a merging that can happen. I never wanted that, but here we are. I think about the sheet with the hole, imagine it covering my whole body. I imagine it covering me right now, and go downstairs to meet Henry where he is waiting for me with that look he gets.

The Owl People

From a distance, the first thing I noticed about Claudette and her husband Ezra, is they both seemed to radiate a lightness of being. They'd recently moved into my building: a smart, brick two-story with large windows. They lived in the apartment above mine, and even before I first officially met them, something compelled me to linger in the hallway, hoping for a brief encounter.

Another thing I noticed right away, based on the quiet from above, is they took off their shoes when they got home, something I'd always had a slightly critical attitude towards, but have started to admire. I'd thought shoeless households were a foolish attempt to try to keep the grime of the world away. My philosophy was more to let all the muck in and get stronger for it. But now I imagined their clean feet, housed in cotton, how they must skate across their polished floors and maybe even hold each other and dance sometimes. The low hum of their music trickled down to me in the evenings. I don't know how to explain it, but even then, I wanted to be near them. I would come to notice the way Ezra held himself, so secure in his body, like no trauma had ever touched him, and I would admire his kind eyes, but it was Claudette who would pull me like a magnet.

Back in my own apartment, the floors were scuffed by my son Remy, whose favorite thing to do was to set up obstacles to jump over, and then run at top speed from room to room, timing himself. Sometimes this was tiresome to me, but mostly I appreciated his independence and animalistic delight. I was forty when I had him; sometimes it takes us queers longer to remember about things like having babies.

At the store, at restaurants, and on the street, I get *ma'am'd* and *sir'd* with equal regularity. I've noticed people are generally quick to categorize others, uncomfortable with ambiguity. When I was younger, starting around age five, people generally assumed I was a boy. I think it's the aging—now that I'm middle-aged, everything is softening, and that causes people to linger on the feminine. And when I speak, all bets are off. Several friends of mine take testosterone, and over the years their voices have taken on a low, prehistoric timbre. Their bodies developed into shapes with more angles, wider backs, and harder stomachs. I never wanted to inject myself with hormones though, sure that with my luck I'd get the worst side effects: acne, balding, and patchy hair sprouting up on my shoulders. And besides, I like existing in the in-between, not quite fitting. On a rare really good day, I might even describe myself as enigmatic.

So I have my faded trucker hats and my effeminate voice, and often people do not know what to make of me. Because of all this, and the fact that I had been single (for all practical purposes) for a while (since I wouldn't be mentioning my recent sexual encounters that could most accurately be described as disastrous entanglements), I wasn't the best candidate in the eyes of most adoption agencies.

So I took out a loan, and headed to the sperm bank in Eugene. The donor I picked out from the catalog had a master's degree and a mischievous grin. His father had been from Ghana, his mother from Sweden. My own father was mixed-race as well, but he died from alcoholism before I got around to asking him about our ancestry. Even though I'm a quarter black, my skin is white like the inside of an almond and my curls only come out after a long swim. I thought this donor choice might, in a strange way, keep our lineage cohesive somehow.

The first time I actually came face to face with Claudette and Ezra, we were all entering the building at the same time. I was nervous to speak to them, with their lightness of being, their clean floors, and the playful dancing I'd imagined, but I didn't want to waste any time with my own shyness. Sometimes—more and more lately—I was able to rise above my own insecurities.

"Oh hi!" I said to them, holding open the door, a churning in my stomach, "I think you live in the apartment above mine. I'm Alex. It's really nice to meet you."

"Great to meet you too!" Ezra said. "We love the apartment. So much light."

Claudette smiled but didn't say anything at first.

"I'm glad to finally meet you," she said after a very long pause, looking at me intensely. That's when I first realized she was an owl. So focused. I couldn't tell what she was focused on exactly, but I found myself wanting to know. I wondered what her "finally" comment had meant, if she'd been curious about me based on something she'd seen from a distance or heard through the floorboards.

Ezra looked at her and then back at me. I realized he was an owl too. Not quite as focused as Claudette, but profoundly good at making eye contact, something I really had to work at. He asked, "So, what do you do?"

I had long ago adopted my mom's working-class stance of bristling when anyone asked that. But I didn't hold this against Ezra. My mom just hated that question, and I guess I did too.

"It's such a capitalistic conversation starter, " she used to say, at our little kitchen table when I was a kid. She wondered out loud why people felt the need to ask that, as if it was the most interesting thing about them. And she wondered why people didn't respond to the question in more creative and interesting ways like, *I try to be kind to people, I believe what children tell me, I like to talk to trees*, instead of which bank or legal firm or clinic they worked at. My mom had worked cutting gloves in a factory until her own hands were almost disfigured. Then there had been a factory fire that resulted in chronic lung problems and she got a settlement.

The other question she hated—for the same reason—and the one that was directed at me growing up, was what I wanted to be when I was older. Adults love to ask a child this question. I told everyone who asked that I wanted to be a marine biologist, specializing in whales.

What I really wanted, but knew better than to say out loud, was to be completely alone living in an igloo in a cold, otherworldly place. I would exist there, happy, hundreds of miles from the nearest human, carefully cohabitating with the arctic hares, the narwhals, and the ringed seals.

"A marine biologist! Specializing in whales!" the adults would say back to me, always impressed.

I had been gone from Claudette and Ezra a little too long, away in my imagined igloo again. This happened to me in conversations sometimes. Unfortunately, it usually happened in conversations that mattered to me the most. I was working on being more focused when I talked to people, but sometimes I floated up and away. Ezra gave Claudette a brief side-glance then turned back to me and said again, slightly louder, "So Alex, what is it you do?"

"I'm a marine biologist," I told him quickly, not having intended to lie, it just came out. I hoped I could still get to know them with this untruth between us. Later that evening, after putting Remy to bed, I realized I hadn't asked them what they did for work, then tossed and turned all night, worried I had been rude.

Over the next few weeks, I saw Claudette and Ezra more often. On the sidewalk or on the stairs. I learned that Claudette illustrated children's books and Ezra was an architect. I found out he did all the cooking, and that they had been training, for fun, to get their pilot's licenses.

Of course they like to fly, I noted, building upon my owl theory.

It was a rainy Saturday morning a couple weeks later that Claudette and I ended up together, alone. Remy had slept over at his friend's house the night before, and Ezra was at the gym. We came into the building at the same time and sat next to each other on the steps, comfortably, as if we had done so many times before. She told me they were from Virginia but had moved to Oregon, needing a change. Both their families were old-money families, and the two of them had been trying to have a baby. Surrounded by their aging parents who were eager to have their first grandchild, and some college friends who already had one or two kids, they had started feeling overwhelmed by the pressure. They needed a break from it all. They would try again, she said, but for now they wanted space to be alone together, just the two of them.

"And here I am now, far from the madding crowd," Claudette said after a long pause.

"Thomas Hardy based that novel on a poem," I said back to

her, grateful to have something slightly notable to add to the conversation. "But distinct from the poem, Hardy wanted to show that quietude and isolated calm were false ideals."

"I couldn't agree more," she said. "I think we humans need each other."

She looked like she wanted to elaborate, but stopped herself. Instead she smiled, abruptly got up, and headed towards the elevator, leaving me wondering yet again. I suddenly thought about my igloo and what a comfort it was to me still; like I could always find my way there if humans got to be too much. Of course I wouldn't ever really be alone now: I had Remy. But he was still young and curious enough that he would see it as a great adventure. I wondered what Claudette would think of my igloo and propensity for solitude.

"Until next time, Alex," she called back to me, smiling a sad smile as the elevator doors opened for her. I wasn't sure, but I had the sense she was on the verge of tears. I wished I'd offered a hug or something, but maybe that would have made it worse.

I don't tell many people this, but sometimes I have visions where I can visit people while they're sleeping and communicate with them. Since sitting on the stairs with Claudette, I hadn't been able to stop thinking about her or Thomas Hardy's perspectives on isolation. Last night, as the visions came, I made my way up the sturdy brick of our building's exterior to Claudette and Ezra's apartment. I sat at Claudette's feet wanting to convey to her that she was an exceptionally special person—she made a difference to people in powerful ways that were below the surface. It wasn't about me. It was about something much bigger and more important than I could explain, even to myself. In our waking life, we hadn't even talked much, but every time I was near her,

I felt more connected to the world, like an unendurable weight was lifted off my shoulders. I had watched her have the same effect on others as well. Remy, for one, often talked about her in a way he didn't talk about any other adults, what she had said in the hallway or how she made people laugh, and asked me a lot of questions about her I didn't have any answers to. Even the building manager, well known for his pinched demeanor, brightened in her proximity. (He was a turkey vulture, his cheeks and nose dark red with rosacea). Claudette was gorgeous but that wasn't what this was about. As the vision continued, I reached toward her, scooped her up in my arms, which were suddenly massive, and lifted her up into the sky. I held her there until each of her muscles, every single one, could just let go for a while and rest.

We floated between some stars for a long time. Her face was so close to mine, almost like we would kiss but it wasn't about that. It was about the thing underneath lips touching, underneath the act of leaning in even: it was about the momentum underneath everything. I heard a sound like a symphony and realized it was our own chasmic laughter as it kept echoing and echoing. When the echoes faded into stillness, I tucked her back into bed, where Ezra snored gently. I leaned over to him, patted his soft, hairy chest, and told him he didn't need to worry. He didn't need to feel threatened in any way, that perhaps Claudette and I would go up and rest in the universe together from time to time. Maybe I would carefully brush the hair out of her eyes or hold her hand, but it wasn't anything for him to feel jealous about, it wasn't about what was happening on Earth, where they were together and in love. It was very important to me that the owls had each other. Later, back in my own bed, curled up under winter blankets, I slept better than I had in a long time.

When I happened to see them the next afternoon, I hoped I wasn't staring too much. I couldn't help but look for some sign of recognition from the night before. Claudette seemed to hold my gaze for just a moment longer than what I would consider normal and I couldn't tell what she was feeling or thinking. Ezra had a bounce in his step and his arm slung happily over Claudette's shoulders. It made me feel good, seeing them like that.

Later in the week, Remy brought a book home from the school library. When I saw it was about owls, I gave him a big hug.

"What made you want to check this one out?" I asked him. He looked at me quietly, his eyes so bright and dark. (I think Remy is a white-tailed deer, but it's too early to know for sure).

"I've just been thinking about them a lot lately. Like, how can their necks spin around like that? How do they hear so well with such tiny ears?"

"Good questions," I told him.

We grabbed an old blanket and sat on the couch to read it. The page he liked the best was about vision. Remy had recently become the one who read books out loud to me, sounding out the longer words in his small boy voice. He read that owls have incredible distance vision, their eyes have tubes that are basically binoculars. "A hawk owl can find a mouse up to a half a mile away," he read.

I thought about Claudette and Ezra. I wondered what they saw in the distance, beyond the streets, above the trees, and past the refinery's smokestack. I wondered how their owl instincts had served them already, where it would lead them next.

Lately, I've been having strange visions. I can sit outside at the park and watch people walk by, or pay close attention to the person bagging my groceries, or the woman who delivers our mail, and all I can see is how we are all melting down into the same stuff. We're all just water and bone, held down by gravity. Most of us long for something, and most of us are not sure how to get it, but we keep trying anyway. I know I am different, that my brain works differently. I see things other people often don't notice, and also miss things many people find obvious. I can watch a whole crowd of people waiting for the train and see them as their skeleton selves—keeping quiet or making small talk, getting their tickets ready or reading a book, all in a kind of existential nakedness. Like high viscosity glass, I can see how we are, cell by cell, slowly being pulled back to dirt.

Running into Claudette and Ezra became a part of regular life. I was always glad when our paths crossed. We didn't invite each other over, and we didn't talk too much. Sometimes they seemed happy together and sometimes they didn't, same as everyone. Remy borrowed sugar from them a couple weeks ago when we had started making cookies and realized we didn't have enough. Little neighborly things like that. I hadn't tried to visit Claudette again the way I had before, but I always paid close attention to her in waking life. I hoped that—even though it wouldn't make sense to most people—both she and Ezra knew I cared about them in a way that felt simple and profound at the same time.

Last night, something unprecedented happened: I was the one visited. It was around 2 AM. Claudette tapped on my window. When I opened it, she leaned in slowly and whispered, "You're very good with animals." Then she laughed a low laugh, and it sounded just like the echoes from when we had been together before. "I can do it too," she said, and I stared at her as she fluttered soundlessly off the windowsill, into the cool night.

Making breakfast for Remy a few days later, I heard a sound at the front door. When I opened it, the hallway was empty but on the mat was a small piece of paper with a drawing of a small fox sitting in a field of stars. I stood there and stared at it for a long time, until Remy yelled from the kitchen that the pancakes were burning. I put the drawing in my pocket and all day and late into the night, I took it out and ran my thumb along its soft edges. Long after Remy went to sleep, I sat alone on the couch and held it in my hands.

When I finally went to bed, I closed my eyes and my breathing got deep and steady. I found myself in a vast field of white, standing alone at the entrance to my old igloo. I stood motionless, watching as its edges slowly dissolved back into all the ice surrounding it, until I could barely tell it had ever been there at all.

Each Motion a Promise

Up so early even the dog refuses to lift her head. Lately I've been having nightmares even worse than in childhood—demons and such, I really don't want to get into details. When he gets up, Liam asks me why my eyes look like black holes, and then pats my back and tells me everything is going to be okay. He's only eight, but is wired for compassion, which is a good thing. Or maybe I've parentified him, in which case I'm a worse person than I thought.

I turn fifty this year and keep having the idea I need to reread *The Picture of Dorian Gray*, which I haven't picked up since I was a sophomore at North Salem High. My best friend Kim gave me her copy, then slept with my boyfriend. The boyfriend and I ended up being gay. Kim is probably gay now too. I keep thinking of Dorian because I'm convinced I can feel the shallow recklessness of my past catching up with me. On a really good day I am able to think of myself as a decent person, but not an extraordinary one. When Liam was born, I felt a kind of hope I don't remember ever having experienced before. Just the fact of him made me feel like a better person, almost good. Maybe all babies do that, at least at first. But I don't really feel like that anymore.

These days, Liam likes to sit in the corner of our living room that has the most light, reading books about insects. Sometimes I'll have a second cup of coffee, mindlessly pet the dog, and pretend to read *The Times*, but all I'm doing is watching the way the sun splashes against his face and makes shadows on the wall behind him. He doesn't like it when I stare, but given the choice, that's how I'd spend most of the day.

"Did you know cockroaches can live for a week even if they've been decapitated?" he asks me. "It's because they breathe through spiracles, not noses."

"Weird," I say. "What else are you reading about?"

"Botfly eggs get into human skin with a mosquito bite, then hatch, and start eating through the person's flesh. People say they can feel them moving underneath their skin but they can't do much about it."

"That's incredibly disgusting," I respond, feeling queasy.

"It's just nature," Liam says, and goes back to his book.

Liam's other parent killed herself when he was two, and he doesn't remember her. I had pictures of Lucie up for a while, but as the years went by, I realized the weight they carried felt increasingly heavy. Lucie and I weren't in love anymore when she did it, but were trying to figure things out for Liam's sake. She was seeing a therapist and in a support group, but her mental health was still deteriorating. I know that now, but I was so focused on Liam then that I just thought it would all work out somehow. I had taken Liam up to Washington to visit my parents for a long weekend, and when we got back, I found her in the tub, post overdose, her mouth slack and still. I looked at her tan body, her lean frame, and remembered how beautiful she was, even through this current horror—how attracted I had been to her in the beginning. I realized that over the years I hadn't even seen her as a person anymore, she was just this sad, gray cloud looming in the corners. Her suicide note said, *Make sure Liam knows I loved him. Sorry about everything.*

I guess that's what the nightmares are about: beautiful bodies and the ends to them. This morning the sun is still rising, and I stare out the window, see the ambitious morning walkers as headless cockroaches, heading to the cafe, still thinking everything is fine.

Liam is made of light, but I wonder how long it will take for him to lift his head and notice all the shadows here. I keep petting the dog's back, each motion a promise to see this through, to feel all the horrible things under the skin, and to coexist with them until it is absolutely no longer tenable.

Annihilation for Beginners

My first day of being fourteen came with a knock at the door to our third-floor apartment. It was Douglas, the eight-year-old boy from down the hall. Every time I saw him, my first thought was always to wonder who would name a newborn baby, innocent to the world, a name like Douglas. People should know never to name a child anything that remotely sounds like or rhymes with ass. It'll be over for them before they even get started.

It was late in the morning and he was still in pajamas, hair bunched up in a tangled cowlick.

"Happy birthday, Joe," he said, handing me a lumpy present.

"How'd you know it was my birthday?" I asked.

"I heard your mom telling my mom you were growing up too fast and that she was looking forward to empty nest syndrome."

I think he wanted me to explain what empty nest syndrome is, but I didn't want to.

Douglas had been about five years old when my mom and I moved into this building. It was east of downtown Salem, close enough to the prison to sometimes hear the guards yelling. Even then I got the distinct feeling Douglas was going to grow up to be gay. Besides prancing on his tippy-toes, he just had this beautiful face. The face, I thought, of a future homosexual. His mom was friendly, but distant and didn't seem like the type to stand up to a tyrant. His father was infamous for his strong opinions that had alienated almost everyone on our floor. I didn't know what this foretold for Douglas.

"Walk flatter!" and, "put your fucking heels down, goddammit!" could often be heard in the hallway.

Dear Reader, this is the first thing to do.
Don't think of Joe or Douglas, think of yourself. Feel the slightest bit of vulnerability and stuff it down, use some witty humor to outrun it, if only for a minute longer. Tie a rubber band around your wrist and snap it hard every time you have a feeling you don't like. Don't let yourself grow calloused: move the rubber band so there's always a fresh sting.

In the hallway, it looked as if Douglas had given up on the goals set for him by his father. He bounced up and down, heels distinctly aloft. In his little kid way, he suddenly had to go, and I watched him bound down the hallway in a sugar-cereal trot. He'd used masking tape to affix a scrawled note to the gift.

"To Joe. For you to come play *The Annihilator* with me ANYTIME."

He had given me a video game controller, black and sticky with finger smudges. Strawberry jam.

For my birthday I always went out to eat with my mom. There was this great diner called Sparky's that served breakfast for dinner. I liked the french toast. She alternated between a spinach omelet or poached eggs and hash browns.

This is the second step.
Allow yourself to have the most basic expectations of family and friends, and (spoiler alert) be simultaneously crushed and

vindicated when they let you down. Think of all the ways people have disappointed you and then turn all the possibilities on yourself. Start really believing you are unworthy of any sort of dependable love. Begin the process of letting go of its existence for anyone, least of all for you.

Mom called around five, when she usually got off work. She was a nurse at the city hospital, the one everyone tried to avoid. Once, on a take your child to work day, Mom and I looked down the empty hallway to see a blood-soaked rag that had fallen off someone's gurney or a biohazard cart.

"Well that just about sums it up, doesn't it?" she asked me.

We burst out laughing in that way that sometimes happens when faced with terrible absurdity. This is what I was thinking about on the phone as Mom let me know three ambulances had arrived, and the hospital was short-staffed. One of the patients was a kid Douglas's age with a paring knife through his eye.

"I can't leave any time soon. I'm sorry about the birthday dinner. I'll make it up to you."

"I understand, it's okay," I told her, staring at the wall.

I looked over at Douglas's note about playing *The Annihilator*. Maybe he was lonely and I could spend my birthday doing a good deed, making him feel like he had a friend: someone who wouldn't mention how he walked on tippy-toes, someone who could just let him be.

And now, the final step.
Embrace any strand of disproportionate self-regard you can muster in order to engage with the world. Try to use it for good, even as you are projecting your own fears and anxieties onto others. Place

yourself at the top and be a benevolent force towards those lower than you on the social hierarchy, even though somewhere deep down you sense that you are the lowest of the low. The trick is to practice believing the lies you tell yourself until you've arrived at perfection, which in this case is complete disillusionment.

I headed to Douglas's apartment. When I knocked, Douglas answered the door immediately, like he'd been waiting, listening for the sound of my knuckles on the peeling frame. I followed him to his room where the game was already set up. I plugged in my controller. Douglas didn't say much, bouncing on his bed with excitement, though I could tell he was trying to play it cool.

"So, what's the point of this game?" I asked.

He was suddenly very still.

"Total destruction," he said.

In our shared silence, I wondered how I hadn't seen it. We could destroy ourselves together.

We sat next to each other with the controllers in our hands for what felt like a very long time.

The Parent

Once a month Greta and I have dinner with Katie and Chloe, a couple who have been friends with Greta since long before I met her. I like to call them my "inherited friends." We usually go out for an overpriced dinner, New American with craft cocktails, talk about the kids, tell stories from work, then hug and walk away into the Portland night. Immediately after each of these occasions, I vow never to do it again.

"How many couple selfies do people need to take at an hour-long dinner?" I asked Greta.

She can't go along with my complaints though. She and Chloe have been through a lot as friends and Greta is fiercely loyal.

"She just likes to remember the fun moments," Greta explained.

I started in on another way to criticize Katie and Chloe, but stopped myself because I love Greta and really do try not to be a jerk.

"Well, she may or may not remember the four whiskey sours she just downed," I joked, getting a little laugh out of Greta.

"You're a real asshole," she said to me, grabbing her keys on the way out the door and kissing me on the neck.

I love that about Greta: the easy, irreverent way she handles things. The next day, you can bet the pictures of Katie and Chloe were mood-lighting-filtered to perfection, posted all over social media, along with pictures of their gorgeous sixteen-year-old son, Etienne, doing something impressive.

Our son Jayden is a teenager also, but no one even remotely prepared me for what a repellent human being he would become. Jayden is seventeen and has "anger management issues" and that is putting it lightly. "Overwhelming hostility and violent tendencies" might paint a more accurate picture. He's worse than ever these days, but the thing is, there's always been something wrong with him, all the way back to when he was a toddler. All I know for sure—more than anything else—is I'm not a person who's cut out for raising anyone.

Stay the fuck out of my room you fucking bitch, is a phrase I recently heard yelled right down our very own hallway. I had opened his door—after knocking and waiting for at least a minute—to see if he was ready for dinner.

We took away all his privileges, but what else can you do? At age seventeen he towers over us at 5'11" and seems to be growing a faint but unnerving mustache. Whenever he wears shorts, I'm still shocked by his dark, hairy legs. His bedroom walls are decorated with fist-sized craters punched in everywhere and his window is cracked. I think he hit it with one of the Nerf guns he's had since he was nine and still refuses to get rid of, even though he'll be a senior next year. I offered him twenty bucks to take all the guns to Goodwill last weekend and he rolled his eyes and said, "You don't understand me at all."

He has a point. I've always harbored a fear Jayden will grow up to be a psychopath or an arsonist, maybe both. He has night terrors when he's sick where he sees demons coming towards him, and he's been trying to burn things up since he first learned the word "hot." We have him in therapy but he refuses to talk. Week after week, another $150 goes down the drain as the therapist reports back, "No, he didn't share anything this time, but he was willing to listen to a calming whale song recording for thirty minutes."

"Isn't it ironic that Jayden's therapy sessions make me want to kill myself?" I ask Greta.

"It'll be okay," she tells me and pats my shoulder, no longer willing to engage with me on the tired subject of my pessimism about Jayden. After so many years—years that, overall, I would categorize as nightmarish, Greta has somehow managed to hold out this steady wellspring of hope for him. It's the aspect of our relationship that causes the greatest rift between us. She stayed right there with him the time in fifth grade he called one of his teachers a "dirty whore" in class, and when he slammed our dog's head in the door and showed no remorse. There was also the time he set fire to the wooden swing set in our neighbor's backyard. And so many more incidents. I really can't imagine how it's possible he could turn out okay, but Greta has this intense trust in him, in her parenting process, and in some future result that she alone can see.

Tonight we're meeting Katie and Chloe for dinner again and I'm already dreading it. What really gets to me is how they go on and on all the time about how they're so queer. I guess anyone can say that these days, and I don't want to police anyone, but from my view they are so blatantly normal, even the straightest straight people in the world seem more interesting to me in comparison. They had a traditional wedding—with about a million people— and required matching bridesmaid dresses from a cheap, taffeta emporium based out of Medford. The worst part is they're constantly touching each other at dinner, as though they can't keep their hands off each other, when I know for a fact they haven't had sex in over two years.

As for my other pet peeve, we are guaranteed to get a card with the cutest pictures of Katie and Chloe, and Etienne of course, every year at Christmas. You know they had to go through thousands of images because they self-document every damn minute. The process must take days, maybe weeks. Greta puts the annual card on the fridge when it arrives in the mail, and it's the only time I feel glad my child might grow up to be a psychopathic arsonist, because at least that's interesting.

"Do we really need to put it up again this year?" I ask Greta.

"If they come over, they might wonder where it is. Besides, I kind of like it. They spend a lot of time together as a family. I think it's sweet." She looks at me, probably wondering if I'll finally see them from her perspective, but I just can't.

"What if we make a holiday card, print it on gorgeous paper and send it out in gold envelopes, but the only pictures will be of Jayden bathed in gray computer light playing violent video games with his usual disturbed grimace?"

"You're absolutely impossible," she says.

The dinner place Katie and Chloe choose tonight is a hipster eatery where everyone working looks to be about twelve years old. I make the mistake, after appetizers, and against my own instincts, of telling Katie and Chloe how much I have been struggling with Jayden since we saw them last. I usually try not to talk with them about parenting issues because it only makes me feel worse to divulge anything vulnerable to them. I'm not sure what compels me to share this time; maybe it's just been an extremely hard week and I can't hold it in anymore. I keep thinking things can't get any worse, but time after time, something else Jayden does sends me off the deep end. I tell them what happened last weekend.

"Jayden started a YouTube channel and I found it online. It's about how America's biggest problem is that women keep falsely accusing men of rape, and how girls at his school treat him like shit." I watch their faces. "I'm seriously afraid he's on the path to becoming an incel."

They look back at me with a profound inability to relate, but after a short silence, recover quickly enough to offer some advice.

"What we do," Katie explains in a voice laden with earnestness, "is read a selection of poetry from the book *Gratitude Here and Now* before we sit down to eat dinner. It might help Jayden feel more grounded. I have an extra copy if you want to borrow it."

I feel an overwhelming jolt of compassion for Jayden and all I want to do is stab her with my salad fork.

God, he must feel like this all the time, I think.

"Etienne just loves it," Chloe chimes in.

Something deep in me snaps completely and I cannot tolerate being pleasant anymore. I don't want to be polite or suffer through their superficial groping, and I most definitely do not want to borrow *Gratitude Here and Now*. I burst out laughing like a lunatic—the kind of laughter that only gets worse when you try to tamp it down. Then I'm talking to them in a clear, low voice that doesn't even sound like mine.

"Are you fucking serious?" I ask, and Greta gives me a cautionary, terrified look. "You don't get it—or us—at all. Jayden would brutally murder both of us on the spot with the nearest butter knife if we tried to read Rumi to him at dinner time. And the thing is, I wouldn't blame him. Etienne is boring as fuck. Your marriage is boring as fuck. And these dinners are boring as fuck."

No one is laughing now, not even me. No, I am definitely not laughing anymore. I look at their shocked faces, worry I've finally ruined everything with Greta, and wonder how or if she will forgive me. But in that moment, all I want to do is find Jayden and tell him how much he means to me. Maybe I can get him to go for a drive, fast on the back roads like he likes. I want him to understand that I finally understand something that he understands. I am hellbent on conveying this to him.

I walk out of the restaurant and pull up my collar to the night air, letting myself believe for one moment that maybe redemption is only possible when, like Jayden, we send it all up in a blaze and see who is still there beside us when the ashes settle.

The Red-Eye

I knew something was wrong as soon as I sat down. On my right, a manspreading golfer with a head cold. He wore tight pants and white sneakers with a golf club pin on the front of his shirt. His husky frame and muscular forearms left me with no hope of using the arm rest. On my left, a kid with a scowl who looked to be about ten, traveling alone. The flight attendant brought the boy pretzels and checked in on him a couple more times, leaning over my seat close enough that I could count her neck wrinkles and glean the faint scent of stale perfume and cheap hotel soap.

The kid reeked of stale piss, and his hair was stringy and damp. His breath: rancid meat forgotten on a counter during a heatwave. I tried to cover my nose with my jacket, turned on the tiny fan above me, and looked down the aisle, hoping there was an empty seat I could move to. Nothing. The kid put in two-hundred-dollar wireless earbuds that even I can't afford and flipped open both a laptop and a gaming system. Even with all his digital distractions, he seemed restless—nervous, almost panicky. He kept looking at me sideways.

"I'm Arthur," I said, trying to ease the growing discomfort rising in my throat, but instead of ease, I made it worse. In the increasing awkwardness I realized I'd never introduced myself to someone on a plane before and that I never would again.

"What game are you going to play?" I choked out.

He looked at me, his face a tight grimace, and without saying anything back, pressed the button for the flight attendant to come.

"I wasn't supposed to be seated by a man," he told her when she came over. His voice grating, gravel under car tires.

"My mom promised there wouldn't be a man by me," he repeated, his voice rising. The flight attendant told him she was so sorry, but she hadn't been informed of this particular request. She glanced at me, before turning her attention back to the kid.

"I'm sure he's a real nice guy," she said, nodding towards me and smiling at both of us with a shrug. "I'm right here if you need anything, kiddo. There's nothing to worry about."

She got called to help an older woman struggling to get her luggage into the overhead bin, but tried to reassure him once more.

"I'll be back soon to check on you," she promised him.

The kid turned away from me, fighting tears. His face was gray and contorted like a gargoyle.

"If you touch me, I'll fucking kill you," he said into the window, low enough that I could barely hear.

I didn't know what to say or do. I turned away from him as much as I could, a sick feeling deep in my gut, but the golfer's legs were crowding mine and there was really nowhere to go. Hours passed. Turbulence. The golfer slept like a dead man. I kept thinking of responses to the kid in my mind. One part of me wanted to comfort him. The other part of me wanted to obliterate him.

You can calm down little dude, I imagined saying reassuringly. *No one here is going to mess with you.*

Then in the next moment: *You really think someone wants to touch your wrinkly, little urine-smelling dick? Is that what all this is about?*

I felt like a complete monster. Compassion to obliteration, kindness to rage, over and over, and I couldn't seem to stop. I didn't understand it, but within the back and forth I had a vague memory I'd felt like this before but couldn't place when or where. It was exhausting. Eventually I drifted off with my neck at an uncomfortable angle. I dreamt of a strange man wearing a red hunting jacket—when he reached his large hands out towards me, I flinched, nauseous and unable to scream or run or fight.

Almost to La Guardia, I was awakened by the sharp smell of ammonia. The kid had peed all over himself, on his seat, and onto mine somehow. I rang the call button and the flight attendant came over. I gestured towards the dark stain, not wanting to wake the kid up. She looked bewildered in the harsh glow of the plane's LED lights, stars out the window. She shrugged.

"I'm not sure what I can do about that right now," she whispered, backing away with practiced sympathy on her face.

When we finally landed, it was six AM and the sun was burning through the haze to greet us. The kid woke up, and quickly put his hoodie over his lap to hide his accident, embarrassed. As I grabbed my backpack and stepped into the aisle, I felt compelled to speak to him once more.

"Not all men are going to hurt you," I told him, a hollow attempt at reassurance.

He looked at me with his tired, red eyes, and then turned back towards the window. He brought his knees up to hug himself into a tight knot, not for a second believing me.

Zeus's Fear

The other day my grandson Cody relayed a story he read about how Zeus feared that humans were becoming powerful enough to take over Mount Olympus. They were whole and mighty with their four arms and four legs, so he split them into two halves, which became the two sexes. Apparently, this is the basis of the "looking for your other half" myth. Cody is fifteen, has braces, and thinks no one will ever love him like that. But what I take from this myth is that androgyny is what was threatening: accepting all that is male and female about ourselves creates understanding and true strength.

What could be more powerful? Zeus knew the splitting would wreak havoc, and it has. Our binary notions suffocate humanity with a vast blanket of our own anxieties.

Cody calls me Pops and practically has to be beaten with a stick to get off his video games. I infuriate him by always choosing a female character when I play with him, which is less and less often these days, even though I'm committed to proving my point. My thumbs are no match for his thumbs. I guess this has always been true, but lately I've started to care. Things aren't working like they used to, but I try to keep my sense of humor. Even through his teen angst, I can still get a crooked smile out of him sometimes. Except with this Zeus story. He doesn't like my androgyny theory. He likes the rules and finds my tiny attempts at sabotage exasperating. He doesn't remember when he was five and only wore leggings and skirts to school. And pink rain boots! That continued for two years! Now he's very attached to his narrow view of masculinity.

When he's not around, I prefer wearing dresses and skirts, flowy things I've acquired on trips. Lately I find myself wanting to parade in front of whatever screen he's on in the most colorful getup I can put together. I wonder if he'd even notice. My son, Cody's father, knows I like to "dress up" (that's what he calls it) and he does not approve. I like to call it simply "being myself." Regardless, he asked me not to share this part of myself with his only son.

The other day though, stopping by after school, Cody asked me to play a video game with him and I did. I chose a character I've named Tabitha who wears a red, purple, and mint green dress, similar to one I brought back from Oaxaca in the seventies. Tabitha slits dragons' throats with an easy swipe.

"She's cool," Cody said, not looking at me directly. "She can really fight."

"I just like her dress," is all I said.

I was anticipating one of his benign but tiresome eye rolls, but Cody instead smiles one of his easy, kind smiles. I smile too, turning away from him to stare ahead at the screen, and wonder if—somewhere deep inside, or even more on the surface—he remembers those pink rain boots after all, and the way they held his small, determined feet.

School of Velocity

Frances, who goes by Frankie, comes to his piano lessons without complaint. His gay moms, who I suspect wanted a daughter, gave him a girl name in the hopes he wouldn't grow up to be a misogynist. I'm pretty sure they hired me as his piano teacher just so he would have an effeminate role model. At first, he was as average as all my other students, fumbling through notes and chords and sneaking glimpses at the clock, but after just a few months he can play pieces that take most people his age much longer to learn.

The thing about Frankie though, is he has some strange habits. He knocks on the door the same way every time, two knocks quick, then three slow. And before he plays, he taps each of his hands to his knees and then swings his legs twice on each side. I don't often focus too much on students' personalities—just their musical education—but there is something about Frankie.

"Did you know that in the sixties and seventies there was a serial killer known as Big Ed Kemper who would kill girls and then cut them into pieces and then have sex with them?"

"Where did you learn about this?" I ask him, a knot growing in my stomach.

"The internet?" he says, his voice rising, not meeting my eyes.

Frankie is eight and often wears a bowtie. His parents are average dressers so I'm not sure how he's so dapper as a third grader. Sometimes when I see him, I think he looks like an uptight little man from the 1920s. It's strange that certain faces go with certain times. Like my boyfriend, Milo. He's got one of those wholesome, ox-looking faces from the 1950s, like he's about to go rescue a cat out of a tree.

When Milo and I first met, I called him The Beaver, but he didn't think it was as funny as I did. Milo is thirteen years younger than me—so while I used to watch *Leave it to Beaver* after school when there was nothing better on—I realize it's possible he has no idea why I was calling him that.

Milo and I often don't get each other. Like this thing that happened with Frankie last week. We started his lesson (knees tapped, legs swung) but he stopped in the middle of his warm-up exercises. I am having him study Czerny's *School of Velocity*, a collection of pieces that help students at a certain level advance with their playing.

He said, "When someone is hurting, do you ever want to make them hurt more?"

I had no idea what to say to that and turned to the next page of Czerny. But he wouldn't let it go.

"Like with Big Ed," he persisted, "he really liked the feeling of hurting people."

He said it as fact—something he'd spent time thinking about.

"Not really sure, Frankie. Let's focus on these notes for now."

We made it through the lesson but I felt uneasy, the knot clenching in my stomach again. When I told Milo about it, he seemed unbothered.

"That's just kid stuff," he said.

When Milo is unbothered by something, he never wants to keep talking about it.

At Frankie's next lesson, I decide to tell him a little more about Czerny.

"He was a child prodigy," I tell him. "He memorized all of Beethoven's works and each week he played them on command at Prince Lichnowsky's palace. All he needed was the opus number called out, and he could play whichever piece without missing a single note."

"Big Ed Kemper was 6'9" and was a prodigy too. His IQ was 145."

Suddenly, I feel like everything is moving too fast, that I can't keep up. I look at Frankie but think of Milo, imagine Ed Kemper's enormous body standing over me, hear Czerny in my head—everything blurring together. The warm air coming through the window rustles the pages of *School of Velocity*. Frankie doesn't notice. He stares straight ahead at the wall with his back rigid and his jaw set, frenetically tapping and swinging, tapping and swinging, like he'll never be able to stop.

It's a Big World

Xavier turned the music up on his phone, earbuds dangling like dejected antennae, mouthing the words with his full lips. He was turning sixteen in a week, and shared the same birthday with his grandfather Lewis, who would be ninety. Xavier loved his grandfather but considered him irrelevant, a benign body whose main activities seemed to be cursing at the squirrels that ate the sunflower seeds out of the birdfeeder each morning, and tinkering with some small project around the house every afternoon. Lewis liked to feel useful.

Lewis did not consider Xavier irrelevant. He had closely watched the boy grow up and had observed the changing times through him, but found he had great difficulty expressing his emotions—they seemed at turns overwhelming and superfluous. Hugging Xavier used to be easy, but as he aged, affection felt more and more like a long, unsteady bridge, too much effort to walk across. Too far—better just to rest, safely.

And there was the almighty phone. Lewis saw how it consumed his grandson, made him into a sort of zombie who didn't even seem to inhabit his body, even put off peeing until he had to stop scrolling and run at breakneck speed to the bathroom. Lewis saw how his grandson laughed more watching a video on the tiny screen than with any actual humans. Lewis conceded he didn't have the insight that seeing Xavier at school with friends might afford, and how he might be different with people his own age. Sometimes he imagined Xavier in the quad, talking to his peers—sturdy, lithe boys with the sun on their faces. He imagined how they might slap each other on the back and laugh together. This vision soothed him deeply.

Once, after reaching a terrible precipice of missing Xavier even though he was right there, Lewis suggested he put the phone down. Trying to be tactful, he said, "The world is so big, and that screen is so tiny."

Xavier looked as angry as Lewis had ever seen him and replied, "You don't get it, Grandpa. Things are just better with this."

Xavier held up the phone with a shrug, and Lewis admitted to himself that indeed he did not get it. He never brought it up again.

Over the past year, Xavier's visits had become more infrequent and more distracted. Lewis blamed the phone. He developed a secret fantasy in which he took the butt of a heavy military knife he kept on the mantel and smashed it down hard onto the glass face of the phone with all its colorful squares—hearing the satisfying crack the screen might make. Instead, when Xavier wasn't looking, Lewis just watched him quietly, how his face lit up so exquisitely in its eerie light. He wondered if the pleasure-making chemicals released in the body were different if derived from human contact or from the digital realm. For Xavier's sake, he hoped they were the same, but the thought made him want to cry, something he had not done in over thirty years.

Lewis had occasionally wondered how he might die, but didn't think about it too much: he was relatively fine with surprises. He did wish for something undramatic and private—no falling on the sidewalk, no car accident downtown.

When the heart attack started, he was seized with terror, but then heard a quiet, inner voice say simply, *yes*.

Xavier was nearby on the couch, earbuds in. The whole family would be coming over the next day to celebrate Lewis and Xavier's birthdays, and Xavier had been tasked with bringing over some supplies early.

Lewis could feel his heart constrict and release, his neck tighten, the pain in his arm pulse. He wished he had crossed that long bridge towards his grandson when he had the chance, however wobbly. He wanted closeness and connection now more than ever, and he gravely wished he had tried much harder. Certainly this was the adult's responsibility? It was too late now. He closed his eyes tight against the pain. He wanted to reach his grandson somehow, across the widening divide, but he didn't know what to say.

"It's a big world!" he cried out suddenly, his throat hoarse with need. "It's a big world!"

But he wasn't able to know if his grandson had even heard, or what meaning, if any, he might make from it.

The Vulture

"See that vulture?" asks the new kid. "The one in the tree?"

I do see it. Its black body brings Edgar Allan Poe to mind. I nod at this child, who looks at me with pale, green eyes.

"What about it?" I ask him, not sure where this was going.

"That's my daddy," says the kid. I kind of understand.

I watch the vulture with him for a while, it's hunched on a low branch, body still, settled into itself. I can see the appeal. Something tough and solemn, ugly yet impressive. Pretty daddies are not in high demand here.

Is this what abandoned sons do, I wonder. See their missing fathers in the birds, and later on, in other men who will ignore them just as thoroughly?

I've been working at Lambert House for only a few weeks, my first job out of college. We provide housing and therapy for foster kids who have been unable to stay in one place for any length of time, usually those who need 24/7 supervision for psychiatric or medical support. Most kids at Lambert House are tough, but Silas has a soft magic about him that, even at age seven, is rare.

"Well, your daddy has very sharp claws," I say, not knowing if that's the best response. He smiles and holds out his hand.

"My name is Silas," he says. "I know you're sad. It's going to get worse. You'll see."

He walks away toward the basketball hoop where kids twice his size play and doesn't look back.

Silas gets assigned to my caseload and we spend more time together. Even though I've read his chart, the stories he tells me in person make me go back and review his file to double-check my own understandings.

Yesterday, he told me in first grade he got dropped off at school early because his foster mom had to be at work for a 6 AM shift. He entered the schoolyard but there was no one there, so he wandered around the back. He found a man lying on the ground with blood all around him and his dick cut off, placed on the ground next to him.

"That's horrible," I said to him. "Do you think about this often?"

"Not really," says Silas. "I wonder about a vulture though."

"Your daddy the vulture?" I ask, getting my stories mixed up.

"No. I wonder if a vulture came and ate the penis. Vultures scavenge dead things. They play an important role."

"That's true," I say, wishing my mentor was sitting in on this session so someone else could take the lead. As it is, I just sit there following Silas's gaze as he looks out the window.

"Here comes one now," he tells me.

I look out and see a large vulture descending—its gnarled, red head, its long black wings blocking out the sun.

Something Divine

Zachariah touched the stubble of his beard, took off his dress, and got in the bath I had drawn for him. Yesterday started with a breakfast of champagne and ended at the Rainbow Room, with a broken high heel, a splitting headache, and three dollars tucked into my underwear. Whenever we went out, something like this happened. Some kind of depraved gorgeousness and sore stomachs from laughter we couldn't remember.

Our friend Queenie, sober for twenty-seven years and not about to let any worthwhile stories go to waste, came over in the afternoon and refreshed us as to all the ridiculous shit we had done.

"Under the barstools?" we cried. "Why were we under the barstools?"

"I have no fucking idea, darlings," she sighed, laughing and shaking her head. "But today is a new day. Have I mentioned my Twelve-step program meets on Monday nights?"

Queenie had indeed mentioned her Twelve-step program. She had told us numerous times that Zendaya was her higher power—"that delicious little baby, I just want to gobble her up." She tried to persuade us into going by saying, not for the first time, that the nightly meetings in the old church basement were the best cruising in the city and that sitting in that windowless room felt like a moment of truth—that rare kind, the raw kind, the important kind, truth that wakes you up at night or feels like a sharp punch.

Really, when I thought about it, Zachariah and I would probably benefit from a Twelve-step program. We'd just been doing this for so long—this extended youth.

"Queer rights now!" we had chanted, twenty-five years ago, out of college and working shit jobs, eating, breathing, and pissing activism. We could see no other worthwhile way to spend our time. It was all very idealistic, very European, very Simone de Beauvoir, very Frantz Fanon, though neither of us had actually read their work, just screen-printed their faces onto t-shirts and knew enough to sound smart at parties.

We did eventually read their work, we grew up, we got jobs that paid and helped our parents worry less. We have always partied though, that has never stopped, and lately I wonder where it's all going and for what. Zachariah shows no signs of slowing down, and sometimes in my dreams I'm in a hamster wheel running and running, but I don't know how to get off.

King Night is when all the drag kings come out, all those queers with their breasts strapped down, all that swagger. The Rainbow Room owner hosts it on Tuesdays, a dead night, just another reminder that misogyny reigns supreme. What would de Beauvoir say? I have some idea.

Just the other night Queenie, Zachariah, and I were sitting there, cocktails in hand. I couldn't keep my eyes off this one king, tall and lean, introduced over the scratchy mic as Levi, wearing too much denim (true to form), possessing a voice like an angel. Like really, an angel. Hearing them jolted something divine in me.

"I think I'm having a spiritual experience," I whisper-yelled to Queenie next to me.

"We all are, honey," she said, and it was true. The room was quiet for maybe the first time in its history: everyone was rapt.

Getting up the next day, something felt different but I couldn't pinpoint what exactly. Finding my glasses on the nightstand, I quietly left the bedroom—it was still dark out—and sat on the front steps in the cool, fall air, drinking warm water with lemon (my morning ritual to detoxify from whatever rotating menu of terrible things I had put my body through the night before). Everything was quiet except for a whirring in my own mind. *Depraved decadence*—a vague phrase that kept presenting itself at the front of my forehead where my headache was the worst. Catching my breath, the throb of my mind kept getting stronger until it solidified into a word, a name actually: *Levi, Levi, Levi.* I felt a dull ache somewhere in the center of myself, downed the rest of my lemon water and went back inside to make coffee.

Our neighbors came over a few weeks later, Selene and Michael. They once told us, early on in our friendship, everyone shitfaced in the backyard under a set of swaying swing lights, that Michael could only orgasm if Simon and Garfunkel was playing. Zachariah and I have seen and done so many things, but that was the most scandalizing news we'd heard in years.

"Wait, you're being serious right now?" I'd asked, down to only ice in my cocktail glass. I didn't mean to shame them, I just needed to be sure what I was hearing.

It's a thing that happens with straight people sometimes—they don't want to be perceived as boring and share things that they never would in less mixed company.

For weeks afterwards, when one of us was DJ-ing in the car on the way to the beach or the grocery store, we'd slip in "Bridge Over Troubled Water" or "The Boxer" and barely be able to contain ourselves, making fake orgasm sounds and trying not to crash. Even Queenie was scandalized.

"Straight people," she sighed. "You just never know what they're going to come up with next."

Weeks passed and I kept seeing Levi out of the corner of my eye, but it was never actually them. Once in line at the grocery store. Once stopped at a traffic light. One night I woke up from a dream in a cold sweat—us in a duet together, glittering in matching black—sleek like techno wolves. In reality I can't sing at all, that is Zachariah's specialty, but in the dream, Levi and I were belting out the most exquisite song together and the crowd was eating it up.

I was and wasn't surprised when I went to the Rainbow Room last night—to have a ginger ale and sit there, tired from work but not wanting to go home yet, just wanting to exist in the dusk of the day, in a crepuscular haze of my own making—and saw Levi, the actual Levi. I kept kind of looking over like a creep, then realized I should just say hi and scooted myself down to order an actual drink, a convenient excuse to move closer. I was full of butterflies and the ginger ale wasn't going to cut it.

"Was that you performing here last month?" I asked, even though I was sure it was.

Levi looked over, thick eyelashes and just-conditioned hair laying atop their head in a wholesome pouf.

"Oh yeah, that was me. Usually people don't recognize me from a performance—all that excessive masculine posturing, and then I shrink down to this," they told me, looking down at their own body, which made me look down at their body. I felt like a creep again.

My drink arrived, scotch and soda, and I took a tentative sip. Levi ran their hand through their hair and took a deep breath. I realized they had deep circles under their eyes, their fingernails bitten down to jagged edges.

"Are you okay?" I asked.

Levi was quiet for a minute. Maybe deciding whether or not to answer honestly.

"Yeah, I think so. Just a little stressed out, I guess. My kid's pediatrician said I had to start brushing her skin. We've been doing it for a few days now. It's called 'dry-brushing.' I don't know, I think I'm just overwhelmed."

I'd heard of this. An ex-boyfriend's sister had a son with autism and they brushed him too. I wasn't sure what to say. The only person I'd ever nurtured at all was Zachariah, and he didn't need any brushing.

"You don't look old enough to have a child, but I guess you must hear that a lot."

"Less and less," Levi said, laughing a little bit. "I'm aging exponentially by the second."

I thought of Levi at home, brushing their child's delicate arm, the whoosh of soft bristles. I considered that I might also benefit from being brushed, from being tended to in such a way.

"You know the only thing she'll watch when I brush her?"

"I have no idea what kids like these days," I said, wishing I'd had a cleverer response.

"Rachel Maddow!" Levi said with a deep laugh. "I don't even watch Rachel Maddow."

"That's a good sign, I think," I told them, picturing it so

easily. Except I saw myself there too, taking turns brushing the child, all three of us watching Rachel Maddow in an easy silence.

The bartender came over.

"Your phone must be dead," he said. "Zachariah called for you on the bar phone. He was worried, wanted to see if you were here. I told him you were fine."

I thought about how many times I'd done this—avoided home—and he never seemed to notice. But this one night, sitting next to Levi with the time slipping away somehow, he sensed something.

"That's my boyfriend," I told Levi. "He's usually not so motherly."

Levi tipped up their almost-empty glass and the ice clinked against their teeth. A favorite song from when I was younger that I hadn't heard in years started playing on the jukebox and my throat went dry. Levi smiled their tired smile.

"I have to get home too. Gotta brush the kiddo before bedtime."

"Good luck," I said and meant it, but it felt like the wrong thing to say.

I wished I had asked more about the brushing, if they had someone to help them with the impossible job of parenting, when they would perform on stage again, about their childhood. There were a million things I wanted to ask, stories I wanted to listen to.

Levi got their card back from the bartender, smiled a small smile, and saluted half-heartedly. They walked towards the front door, then out into the night. I paid and got up to leave but that old song was still playing. I stood on the empty dance floor alone and closed my eyes, swayed to the music, and reminded myself of something I had been starting to forget, running my hands down the hair on my arms: I was here in a body, I was here in a body. I was here.

Push Me Away a Little Closer

Grandad sits in his chair, scowling into space. I've heard all his stories a million times—of backpacking trips over mountain passes, Grandad carrying everything on his back. Or cutting off his finger while making a dollhouse for my mom when she was little, refusing the hospital and wrapping the bloody stump with old gauze.

"It doesn't hurt at all!" he had insisted, or so the story goes.

Everything somehow turned out okay with Grandad, until recently. Now he's still like a boulder, and that heavy. He sucks the air out of the room while we tidy this and dust off that, remind him how to use the microwave, put on smiles.

I go over on my motorcycle twice a week after summer school lets out. Mom gives me twenty dollars for each visit. She has had enough of him, and there's no one else. Grandad gave me the motorcycle when I was only twelve and couldn't ride it. It just sat in the garage tormenting me. Now I'm finally old enough.

"Would you look at that! Your helmet is horrendous!" he exclaims when I come in. With last year's birthday money I got myself a helmet the color of a neon orange safety cone.

"I know, Grandad," I say, "I'm just trying to stay alive."

He scowls, like usual. We've had this conversation at least twenty times. Grandad can get pretty mean.

"You're a sissy, not going to amount to anything!" he yells at me this afternoon when his demon cat scratches me out of nowhere and I scream. (I admit I hit a pretty high note.) He and the cat are two old fleabags, peas in a pod.

"Peas in a pod" is something my Grandma used to say. She was the one we all liked best. We always thought she'd live the longest, that we'd have more time with her, but she died last year—an unexpected stroke she didn't recover from.

Now we have Grandad, sunk into his La-Z-Boy, yelling at the TV.

"A parade?! What in the world? That is just goddamn ridiculous."

The news is showing Portland's Pride Parade, where I wish I was. Mom knows everything about how I like other boys, even my crush on Marcos. She's supportive, but says I'm not old enough to go up to Portland with just friends and no adults. Maybe next year when I'm seventeen.

"What I don't get," Grandad says, eyes glued to the TV, "is why the women are so ugly and the men are so beautiful."

More and more often I don't know what to say to him, and it's exhausting to stay positive. Lately, I try to amuse myself to pass the time.

"You find the men attractive?" I ask, smiling.

I am expecting a big protest but he just looks at me. He looks at me closely, maybe more closely than he ever has. I wait for criticism, for some kind of onslaught. He just sits there looking me over.

"I'm sorry," he says. "For everything."

I'm not even sure he's talking to me, but I don't want to ruin this moment. He leans over in his chair and motions me toward him for a hug, something he hasn't done since I was seven or eight with a scraped knee or bumped head.

I wrap my arms around him and for a second I feel better than I have in a long time.

"Are you wearing perfume, sissy boy?!" he yells, pulling away from me and pinching his nose dramatically.

I straighten up to stand and pat him on the back, pick up my helmet, and head towards the door.

"I'll see you again on Thursday, Grandad," I say.

I look back at him as I start to pull the door closed behind me, see his thin lips tremble. He looks like a little kid for a moment and then, just as suddenly, he's back to his old man self, stomping his foot against the recliner. He starts to change the channel, but then doesn't—he holds the remote in the air like he's a conductor. He keeps watching the celebration, all those gorgeous men on the TV in their exquisite plumage—all those beautiful, bright birds, just beyond his reach.

ACKNOWLEDGMENTS

Thank you to the editors of the following publications in which versions of these stories were previously published:

Beyond Words, Electric Literature, The Flexible Persona, The Forge Lit, Gold Man Review, io magazine, New World Writing, Obelus Journal, Peculiar Journal, Prometheus Dreaming, Querencia Press, The Racket, Rappahannock Review, Saints and Sinners Anthology.

Thank you Emmi, Ellen, and Edy at Buckman Publishing. It has truly been a pleasure doing this project together. Hillary, my beautiful, wise, and mischievous friend—how would I make it here on Earth without you? (I wouldn't). Kevin and Carla, our strange literary threesome is a delight. Dusty, thanks for all these years of supportive check-ins and photographic reports from throughout the west. Kim and Clark, your brains and hearts could take down an entire empire, huzzah! Stephany, Jade, and Lewis, you're my gayest and most lovely San Francisco darlings. Anna, your very small skeleton feet will never be forgotten and I hope you always swear at least once during book club. Bev, thanks for protecting Sea Wolf Books with your powerful Gestalt spells, witchy dancing, and enthusiastic day-drinking. Jenny, cutest friend since age three, even across all these mountains and prairies and rivers. Robin, thank you for garden time, forest hangouts, and very impressive animal impersonations. Kali, homesteading hero, I kind of just want to live in your kitchen. Kait, your thoughtful handwritten card came last summer right when I needed it most. Thank you, Travis, my smart and smart-ass philosophical long-lost brother. Faraci and Janae—adorable and fun adventure pals—I love how you both show up for it. Fern and Heather, very fond of your bookstore visits and our road trips to The Spoon. Julianna, thank you for this beautiful book art and your friendship these last few decades—I love our emotional collaborations that always happen at exactly the right time. Mom and Grandma—you're the best parts of this place and me. And beloved Oregon, I will always be in awe of your vast ambit of green.

ABOUT THE AUTHOR

Born and raised in Oregon, Charlie J. Stephens (they/them), has lived and worked all over the U.S. as a bike messenger, wilderness guide, high school English teacher, and seasonal shark diver. Charlie's debut novel, *A Wounded Deer Leaps Highest*, was longlisted for The Center for Fiction's First Novel Prize and was a finalist for the Oregon Book Awards. In 2025, it was awarded the Leslie Feinberg Award in Trans and Gender-Variant Literature and the Bronze Foreword Indies Award for LGBTQ+ fiction. A resident of Port Orford on the southern Oregon coast, Charlie is the owner of Sea Wolf Books & Community Writing Center.

www.ingramcontent.com/pod-product-compliance
Lightning Source LLC
LaVergne TN
LVHW040055080526
838202LV00045B/3641